Taboo

Also by Jess Michaels

A RED HOT VALENTINE'S DAY — ANTHOLOGY
SOMETHING RECKLESS
EVERYTHING FORBIDDEN
PARLOR GAMES — ANTHOLOGY

Taboo

Jess Michaels

red

AVON

An Imprint of HarperCollinsPublishers

Rom
Michaels

TABOO. Copyright © 2009 by Jesse Petersen. All rights reserved. Printed in the United States of America. No part of this book may be used or reproduced in any manner whatsoever without written permission except in the case of brief quotations embodied in critical articles and reviews. For information, address HarperCollins Publishers, 10 East 53rd Street, New York, NY 10022.

HarperCollins books may be purchased for educational, business, or sales promotional use. For information, please write: Special Markets Department, HarperCollins Publishers, 10 East 53rd Street, New York, NY 10022.

FIRST AVON PAPERBACK EDITION PUBLISHED 2009.

Designed by Diahann Sturge

Library of Congress Cataloging-in-Publication Data
Michaels, Jess.
    Taboo / Jess Michaels. — 1st ed.
        p. cm.
    ISBN 978-0-06-165771-9
    1. Aristocracy (Social class) — England — Fiction.   I. Title.
PS3613.I34435T33   2009
813'.6 — dc22   2008044736

09 10 11 12   OV/RRD   10 9 8 7 6 5 4 3 2 1

For *Andrea Williamson,*
one of the nicest friends or fans that a girl could ask for,
with much appreciation and affection.
And for Michael.
The reasons could fill a book in themselves.
I'll just have to recite them to you later.

Chapter One

The Earl of Blackhearth, Nathan Manning, had once considered the heat of a summer's day in India to be stifling. But now, after waiting in the parlor of his great aunt's London home for almost half an hour, surrounded by his mother and two younger sisters, he truly understood what it meant to be stifled. At this point, he would prefer July in India on the back of an unwashed elephant. Anything but this.

And yet he had no choice but to be back in England.

"Nathan, your aunt has been tittering all week about your visit," his mother said with a conspiratorial smile at his sisters, Adelaide and Lydia.

Nathan arched a brow and gave his mother a look that could not be misinterpreted. His aunt, Lady Worthington, was not a woman prone to "tittering" over anyone. And Nathan had clear memories of her once berating him quite savagely when he was a child. He had never been her favorite.

But when the prodigal son returned, it seemed he was remembered as *everyone's* favorite. Which was why he had been paraded around all week, giggled over, pinched, and basically treated like a piece of meat—rich meat that would soon set out to find a wife.

Before Nathan could answer his mother or she could react to his look, the door to the parlor opened and his aunt stepped inside. Nathan got to his feet to greet her. Just as he recalled, she was a tall, thin, stern woman with little light or joy in her expression.

Still, she spared the group with a small, tight smile before she said, "Do forgive me for making you wait. I was just finishing up with my seamstress. I shall return momentarily."

Nathan suppressed a yawn and turned away from the door to pace the small parlor. Outside, he heard his aunt speaking to someone, her strong voice coming in clear into the parlor.

"Thank you so much, Miss Willows, for your help. I much look forward to seeing the gown."

Nathan stopped pacing and lifted his head. Miss Willows? No, it couldn't be. It wasn't. There was no way it could be . . .

"You are more than welcome, Lady Worthington. I shall be certain your dress is ready long before the ball."

Nathan spun around, the voice of the other woman piercing into his body, penetrating his very soul. He found himself moving toward the door, almost against his will. When he reached the barrier, he stopped, peering into the foyer that was just a few feet away.

And there she was—Cassandra Willows. Just as he remembered her from four years earlier. Except more beautiful, if that was even humanly possible.

Her dark auburn hair was bound against the nape of her neck and little strands fell around her face. The face that had lost some of its innocent roundness, the fullness to her cheeks. Now it was quite slender, her pale skin luminescent, and the freckles he had fallen in love with were long gone.

And her dress. No longer did she look like the daughter of a middle-class merchant. Her clothing was the height of fashion, fitted perfectly to her full breasts, then sweeping down dramatically over her form.

Nathan opened his mouth, but found he had been rendered speechless as he stood staring at a woman he had not seen in four years—a woman whose voice he'd last heard telling him she loved him . . . right before she did not show up for their planned meeting. Right before she reneged on her agreement to run away to Gretna Green and threw him over for another man.

In that moment, there were so many emotions bombarding Nathan that he could scarce name or place them all. But two exploded to the forefront, making themselves known in powerful, almost equal measure.

The first was lust, a need that heated his blood to a surprising level and made his hands shake with a desire to reach out and cup the swell of those luscious breasts. He was startled by a powerful drive to feel this woman writhe beneath him in ultimate pleasure as he claimed her again and again.

The second was anger. Anger he had tried to tamp down and deny during his years away in India. It was a strong emotion he thought he'd mastered until this moment, when it washed over him in a wave that threatened to drown him. This woman had lied to him, betrayed him, and played him for a fool.

And for some reason, he still gave a damn about that fact, even after all this time.

"That sounds perfect, Miss Willows, I shall see you then," his aunt said with a smile that was far warmer than those she gifted to most people.

Cassandra opened her mouth to reply, but then stopped. She turned slightly, almost as if she sensed his stare burning through her clothing. Her gaze slipped to Nathan, standing in the doorway like a fool. The moment stretched out between them for what felt like an eternity, though in reality it was little more than a few seconds. All the blood left Cassandra's already pale cheeks, she swallowed hard and blinked a few times.

But then all the reaction was wiped clean from her expression. She returned her attention to Nathan's aunt. "Good afternoon, Lady Worthington."

Without so much as a second glance in his direction or a word of acknowledgment for his presence, Cassandra turned away and departed the house. Nathan could do nothing but stare at her retreating back until his aunt's servant shut the door behind her.

"Great God, Nathan, you look as though you've seen a ghost. Have I changed so much during your years in that savage country?" his aunt snapped, as she grasped his arm and almost dragged him back into her parlor.

"O-Of course not, Aunt Bethany," he stammered, finding his voice with much difficulty. "I was simply admiring your fine home."

"Bah." His aunt blessedly released his arm from her claw-like fist and motioned for the rest of his family to retake their seats. "You were staring at me while I spoke to Cassandra Willows about my gown."

Nathan swallowed hard at the mention of Cassandra's full name. He shot a sidelong look at his mother. Though his aunt and his sisters might not have any idea of the connection he had once shared with the popular seamstress, his mother was fully aware. Shifting uncomfortably, she managed to keep a bright smile on her face, even though it didn't quite reach her eyes.

"You are having Miss Willows design your gown for the soiree?" Nathan's sister Adelaide said with a sigh of pure delight. "Oh, I have seen some of her creations and they are divine! Mama, why have you never employed her services?"

Nathan arched a brow as he waited for his mother's reply, curious as to how she would respond. She had been as against the match between he and Cassandra as his father had been, though perhaps less vocal.

"Yes, you really should, Philippa!" Lady Worthington continued with a rap of her hand against the arm of her chair. "She is a marvel with silk."

"Oh, yes!" Nathan's other sister, Lydia, cooed. "Please do, Mama. Fiona Grey would *die* if I had a Cassandra Willows creation and she did not."

Nathan's mother slowly rose to her feet, patently refusing to make eye contact with him. "That is hardly a reason to employ a seamstress, Lydia. And I've never been quite as taken by Miss Willows as the rest of the *ton* seems to be."

"Oh, Mama!" Lydia wailed.

Nathan's mother lifted her hand to silence all protests. "Enough, child. Now we should be getting along. I hate to depart so quickly, Aunt, but we have other calls to make this afternoon."

Lady Worthington got to her feet with a grunt of displeasure. "You have hardly arrived, Philippa."

Nathan folded his arms and watched his mother squirm under Aunt Bethany's hawkish and utterly disapproving stare. It seemed he wasn't the only person still affected by memories of the past.

If only Cassandra had been.

His mother patted their aunt's hand. "I truly apologize, but it cannot be helped."

The older woman's eyes narrowed ever further, but finally she shrugged. "I shall see you at your dinner engagement in a few days regardless."

His mother let out a sigh of relief. "Indeed you shall."

Aunt Bethany turned to Nathan with an appraising look. "It was wonderful to see you again, my boy. You're too tan by far, but I'm certain we'll see you married off before the Season's end. A new face is almost always snatched up. Besides, you need to start providing heirs, don't you?"

Nathan muttered one of the same platitudes he always repeated when his romantic—or lack of romantic—future was brought up by a meddling relative. As his mother and sisters filed from the room, he stayed back for a moment.

"Aunt Bethany," he said, as he took her arm and led her into the foyer where she had stood with Cassandra not half an hour before. He imagined he could still smell Cassandra's perfume hanging in the air. "Do you have a card with Miss Willow's direction?"

His aunt wrinkled her brow, but she snapped her fingers at the butler who stood beside the front door in the parlor. "I do, why?"

Nathan shrugged as he took the card the butler had produced. A high quality one, to be certain, on expensive paper and with gold foil lettering. It seemed Cassandra was doing as well as his spies had reported over the years.

"My sisters seem quite taken with the idea of having her design something for them," he explained, as he placed the card into his breast pocket. "And since my mother seems immovable on the subject, perhaps *I* shall call upon the lady."

"She runs a fine business, very busy, especially this time of year when the flock returns to London and starts getting itself into a snit over which gowns they should wear." His aunt rolled her eyes. "But I'm sure she will make time for a powerful man such as you."

Nathan could hardly contain his smirk as his aunt motioned toward the door and the waiting carriage. "Good-bye, my boy."

He nodded his farewell and made his way to the carriage and the next tortuous stop with his family. But for the first time since his return to London, he was distracted from his ennui. In fact, he felt alive.

As the carriage began to move, he patted the pocket where the card lay. Cassandra Willows would make time for him, of that he was certain. After all, they had much unfinished business.

Cassandra Willows stood in the large parlor that she had long ago converted into a sewing studio and stared at a beautiful piece of blue silk stitched with perfect white roses. With a sigh, she drew out her measuring tape and did yet another calculation.

"Measuring again?" her friend and assistant, Elinor Clifford, asked as she lifted her gaze from the overflowing calendar of appointments she had been reviewing.

Cassandra clenched her teeth. "I mismeasured Miss Tensley's gown not half an hour ago, and I shall have to absorb the cost of replacing the silk myself. I do not wish to make the same mistake twice."

Elinor shook her head and returned her attention to her own task. "I've never known you to make that mistake once, let alone twice."

Cassandra chose not to answer her friend. There was no use in responding, for she couldn't reveal the truth to Elinor even if she wanted to. She couldn't tell anyone that the reason for her distraction was that she hadn't stopped thinking about Nathan Manning since the moment she saw him at his aunt's home yesterday.

She shivered at the memory of him standing in the parlor doorway, staring at her with such a cold, dismissive air. It had taken all her strength and presence of mind to simply turn away as if she hadn't recognized him.

No one could ever know the past they shared—the passion, the love, and the heartbreak that had torn them apart in the end and made Cassandra realize how little regard the man truly had for her.

"I must be off and check on that special order of thread you placed last week."

Cassandra heard her friend's words, but they didn't fully pierce the fog of her mind.

"Cassandra?" her friend asked, tilting her head in concern. "Are you quite well?"

"Very fine, thank you," Cassandra lied, as she shook off her thoughts and began to cut the expensive fabric before her. "I am very busy, but it is always this way at the beginning of the Season. I'm certain all will be calm and normal again soon."

Elinor closed the calendar and rose to her feet with a sniff of discord. "Perhaps, but I still say you are running yourself ragged. Between this business and your . . . *other* one, you hardly sleep at all. I worry . . ."

Cassandra cut her off with a wave of her hand. "I appreciate your concern, but it is unnecessary. I know my limits."

"Do you?" her friend asked, as she exited the room. "Sometimes I wonder."

Cassandra watched as her friend departed, only to be replaced by the butler who was coming through the door. "What is it Wilkes?"

"You have a visitor, Miss Willows," the servant said.

"If this person does not have an appointment, tell them they will have to return later," she sighed as she looked at the mountain of fabric on the table across the room. "I am behind as it is."

Mostly because she had spent the previous evening mooning over the past rather than working. A fact she didn't share with the servant.

"I did mention that you saw clients by appointment only, Miss Willows," the butler continued and he was beginning to look distressed. "But the gentleman is insistent, almost threatening. He refuses to give a name or to leave until he has an audience with you."

Cassandra paused for a long moment before she set her scissors aside and sucked in a breath. A man who refused to leave when asked? Who demanded an audience as if he owned her time? A man with enough power to worry her butler?

Well, that could only be one person, couldn't it?

She smoothed her skirt and fought to remain calm. "Send this 'gentleman' in, Wilkes, if he is so insistent."

The servant nodded and departed to collect the intruder. As she waited, Cassandra took up the fabric she had just finished cutting and examined it. The soft swish of silk against her skin soothed her. Sewing had always had that effect. She needed that calm now more than ever if her guess as to who had invaded her home was correct.

"Good afternoon, Miss Willows," Nathan said, as he walked through the door.

Cassandra set the fabric aside as she got to her feet. She moved a step toward him before she could stop herself.

"Nathan," she whispered. Now that they were alone, she was unable to muster the control she had managed to wield when she first saw him.

He smirked in response to her use of his given name. His eyes—so bright and almost impossibly blue when compared to his dark, tanned skin and black hair—were hard. They weren't anything like they had been when she saw him last four years before. Then they had been illuminated by what she thought was love.

She shook her head, composing herself with difficulty. It was her only choice. "I assumed you would come here at some point, my lord."

"You thought I couldn't stay away?" he asked, folding his arms across his chest. His tone was as icy as his gaze.

Cassandra blinked, still mesmerized by the sight of him standing in the midst of her home, her sanctuary. She had dreamed many dreams over the years that were so similar, but normally those ended with something far more passionate than his expression boded. Not that she wanted his touch in reality. That had ended long ago.

"Obviously you are well able to stay away," she said softly. "You have been gone nearly four years."

"And you have been very busy during that time, haven't you?" he said, moving forward one long step and closing the door firmly behind him.

Cassandra couldn't help but let her gaze fall on the now-closed door. A hundred shocking images filled her mind. They were alone, no one would invade upon her privacy. Her servants were well-trained on that score. Despite the impropriety of the situation, a shiver she couldn't suppress worked its way along her spine.

"I have done reasonably well for myself, yes," she answered, chewing her lip nervously.

"Come now, Miss Willows." He moved toward her again, rapidly closing the distance between them. "Let us not have false modesty."

He stopped just inches away from her and Cassandra was forced to tilt her head to look up at him. And look she did. The previous day in the hallway she hadn't dared to stare, but now she could look to her heart's content.

Dear God, but he was still handsome. He always had been, but the years away had made him fully into a man. Hardened him in all the right places, put an edge to his gaze, a harshness to his jaw. But his lips were the same—full and abundantly kissable.

Hot images of every kiss they had ever shared darted through her mind, making her dizzy and achy. With a start, she turned away. There was no use thinking of those things.

"I have been fortunate," she whispered, willing her hands to stop shaking.

She felt him move even closer. He was just behind her now, his hot, hard chest brushing her back, his breath against her neck as he leaned down over her.

"You used your talents well, Cassandra."

Steeling herself to her ragged emotions, Cassandra forced herself to pivot slowly and face the man who had haunted her dreams—her life—for so many years. She stifled a moan as they stood chest to chest, almost touching, but not quite. It was torment to be so close to him—a stark reminder that all her hottest fantasies still starred him.

"Why are you here, Nathan?" she whispered, staring directly into his startling blue eyes, even when she wanted to turn away from his stark disdain.

One corner of his mouth tilted up and she noticed a tiny scar there that stood out faintly against his dark skin. That was new, and she briefly wondered how he had gotten it—a fight, an accident, or maybe some grand adventure?

"Perhaps I wish to order one of your specialties," he said, his voice impossibly hard and rough with anger, but also with what she fully recognized as desire. In some way she was relieved that he felt the same sexual connection that she still did. Even if neither of them wanted it, at least it put them on equal ground.

"You wish to order a gown?" she asked with a smirk of her own. "I think blue would be your color, but I'm not certain you will like this Season's cuts."

Years ago, her comment would have made Nathan smile, but now he didn't react at all. Cassandra felt her heart sink. Things had changed irrevocably. Truly, he did hate her. She had known that for a long time, but seeing the final evidence still stung.

"I don't mean a gown, my dear," he said, his eyes narrowing. "I mean your *real* specialty—those interesting little toys you design for men of the *ton*, their mistresses, and the more adventurous wives."

Cassandra's lips parted in shock. If he knew of her quiet side business, the one that brought in nearly twice as much money as her services as a seamstress, he truly had been watching over her all these years. Her toy designs were done very discreetly, through specific channels in order to protect her precarious reputation.

But now she felt naked and vulnerable. And when Nathan stared at her, a sneer of disdain on his handsome face, she almost felt shameful.

No. She shook away that emotion. In four years, she had never felt ashamed of the work she did, of the fact that she had taken lovers, or of the way she had used her abilities to protect herself and better her situation. She wouldn't allow Nathan Manning to stride into her life and make her feel less worthy because of the things she had done. He had no idea of her life since his departure, no matter how many spies he had hired or accusatory comments he made.

Pushing past him, Cassandra paced back to her worktable and picked up the silk she had been cutting. Pretending to be bored with him, she began to drape the fabric over the model beside her table.

"My schedule is quite full at present, my lord. I have no time for any additional work." She refused to look at him, even though she wanted desperately to see his reaction. "Now, you have seen me and vented some of your anger. I don't think we have anything else to discuss. Please go."

"No."

His answer was so quiet that Cassandra couldn't help but turn back toward him. He stood exactly where she had left him, his arms folded across his muscular chest, his bright eyes piercing through her as though she were the only person in the world.

She shook her head in disbelief. This dark and angry man was nothing like the one she had known four years ago. Nathan didn't even resemble the lovesick boy who had declared he would give up anything to be with her. He wasn't the gentle lover who had carefully introduced her body to pleasure.

And despite herself, she was even more attracted to him now than she had been before. Her body reacted to his overpowering presence of its own accord; her nipples tightening to almost painful sensitivity beneath her fitted bodice, her thighs wet with her arousal.

Suddenly a small smile quirked his lips again, almost like he could read her desires as plainly as she could detect his. And it was clear that her undeniable attraction was a triumph to him, as much as his was to her.

The air between them grew even more sexually charged

and she gasped for breath as her thoughts spun out of control. Even though it was utterly foolish and inappropriate, every part of her wanted to bare her body to him and dare him not to touch her. If she did, would he surrender to his own desire, to the lust that was nearly as obvious as his anger?

"You won't leave?" she asked, hating the tremble in her voice.

He shook his head slowly.

She gripped her hands into fists at her sides. "Why not?"

"Because I am not finished 'venting my anger,' as you called it, not by a long run. No, I'm not going to leave here—leave *you* alone—until I have every question answered to my satisfaction. The first of which being, is *this* what you left me for? This life, is it why you threw me aside like I was garbage? Truly, I want to know."

Chapter Two

*T*he moment he asked the question, Nathan wished he could take the words back. Oh, he did want to know the answer to his query, there was no denying that even to himself, but asking Cassandra so bluntly about her reasons for leaving him only made him seem desperate and needy. The fact that those out-of-control emotions were exactly what he felt was not something he wished to examine too closely.

And there she stood like an ice queen, her expression totally unmoved by him. That made everything he felt all the worse. He so wanted to move her, to make her quake, to make her show him the emotions she had when he first entered her chamber. He wanted to make her hurt and long the same way he did.

"I have no idea what you mean, my lord," she said softly.

He frowned. "Yes you do. Of course you do. Did you abandon our plans to marry so that you could go to London and become the whore of a few rich men? Did you so desperately want to work in trade as a seamstress? Or were the depraved little toys you design your real goal? Was all this," he made a jerky motion around the room with one hand, "worth giving up becoming a countess, and eventually a marchioness?"

"I wasn't with you so that I could be a countess or a marchioness," she hissed. The anger he had been craving lit up her eyes for an all-too-brief moment, and then she stuffed it down, shooed it away. "What is the point of this, Nathan? You shall believe exactly what you wish, you always have."

Nathan frowned, confused by her turn of phrase, but before he could address that, she shook her head.

"It is best to leave the past in the past." She let out an exhausted sigh like she couldn't be bothered by him anymore. "Please, just go away."

Without a further word, Cassandra turned to leave the room—to walk away from him just as she had done all those years ago. Only this time he had the power to stop her. Without stopping to think, Nathan crossed the room to her in a few long steps, caught her elbow, and yanked her around, forcing her to look at him.

There was no resistance in her frame, no stiffening of her body. Her soft curves molded to his as if this embrace were perfectly natural and cordial. Her scent wafted up to him, a heady lilac that made him want to breathe her in.

But that wasn't what broke his last shred of self-control. When he looked down into her eyes, he finally got a glimpse of her soul. No matter what she said or how she tried to dismiss and deny him, burning hot lust boiled in her green stare.

So he took it. Dropping his mouth to hers, he branded her with a kiss that matched the heat of their connection. Without finesse or gentleness, he breached the barrier of her lips and drank in her taste. Fresh mint and orange citrus melded on his tongue and he uttered a groan into her mouth.

She echoed the wanton sound, gripping his lapels in fists as she opened wider, thrusting her tongue to duel with his. He drew her closer, her breasts flattening against his chest, his legs tangling in her skirts as he rocked his body to hers. Beneath his trousers his cock pushed hard, ready and randy to join with her, as if he hadn't had a woman in all the time they'd been apart.

Only one thing marred the experience of touching her again. This wasn't the kiss of the woman he remembered, who had been so shy, so innocent in her passions. This kiss was a reminder that Cassandra had been far from innocent since she threw him over. He *knew* she had been with several men. He'd wager she'd done many a wild and passionate thing with those men.

He pushed her backward toward the chamber wall, his anger at that realization making him rougher, more demanding in his embrace. But it didn't dull the desire he felt. Not in the slightest.

Before he could reach the barrier, before he could lift her

skirts and have what he so craved, Cassandra pressed her palms against his chest and shoved. She staggered away from him a few steps, her breath coming in pants, but she didn't look away. She didn't blush with embarrassment. She just stared at him.

"That is enough," she whispered between gasping breaths.

He shook his head, in no mood for denials—not after so many years. "No, it's not. It's not enough, Cassandra, I want more."

She tried to keep her face stony, he saw her fighting to remain stoic, but she failed. The blood drained from her cheeks and her lips, swollen red from his passionate, rough kisses, parted on a gasp.

"More?" she said, her voice no more than a broken whisper.

Nathan shut his eyes briefly. What he was about to say was utter folly, but it didn't matter. He had been deprived of his desire for too many years, and soon he would not be at liberty to pursue his needs. This was his one chance to purge this woman from his memory. To make sure she knew what she had thrown away. To get retribution in the most pleasurable sense of the word.

When he opened his eyes again, he knew how cold he appeared and how cruel he sounded. "Yes. You see, I am here to find a wife."

An almost imperceptible twitch marred the corner of her lips. So she was thinking about how once she had been his chosen mate, just as he was. Well, those days were long gone.

"Someone from a titled and appropriate family this time,

as the last time my foolishness led to nothing good," he continued with a sneer.

To her credit, she did not react to his taunting. "Well, I wish you luck with that endeavor. But I see no reason why it should have anything to do with me, my lord."

"It doesn't, not this time." He shook his head. "But I do need someone to warm my bed until the time comes for me to make my decision. And that person will be you, Cassandra."

She stepped back, her gaze flitting to his face with pure terror and utter confusion. "What?"

"You know what I said."

"You cannot mean that . . . *want* that!" she cried.

He smiled at her outburst. "You and I have unfinished business. And until I find a proper wife, I demand we settle it. In my bed, until I am bored of you."

Cassandra could scarcely hear over the sudden roar of blood rushing to her ears. She could not speak for the lump that had formed in her throat.

She had to be wrong! To have misunderstood. After everything they had been through, everything that Nathan believed about her, there was no way he could want to have some kind of long-term affair with her.

And yet, when he kissed her it was more than apparent that his desire had just as much heat and desperation to it as her own. She squeezed her eyes shut and tried to block thoughts of that kiss away. It had reminded her so much of all those years ago when she had believed him to be a shining prince who loved her. Now he was more tempting devil than fairytale hero. And his demand that she come to his bed had nothing to do with love.

Rather, his crass command was all about vengeance. His desire for her was equaled only by his disdain. Both radiated from him as he stood staring at her, awaiting her reply to his shocking directive.

Cassandra ignored his impatient stance and drew in a few long breaths. In the time they had been apart, she had faced a great deal and she'd done it all alone. From experience she realized she had to remain calm and be rational, or she would reveal even more weakness than he had already seen and he could use it against her.

She folded her hands in front of her. "After everything that has happened, you *cannot* be serious in this request."

He laughed, but it wasn't the rich, sensual sound she re-membered. It was bitter and hard, lacking in all warmth and true humor. She fought the urge to wince.

"When it comes to sex, I am always serious, my dear," he said with an arched brow. "And it wasn't a request, it was a statement. You *will* be in my bed. For as long as I desire you to be there."

The façade of her calm couldn't help but be chipped by his arrogance. She folded her arms tighter and clung to control with everything she had.

"How can you make such an assumption that I would sim-ply bow to your will, my lord?" she asked through clenched teeth. "Certainly, I have proven that I am my own woman in the past."

His nostrils flared and she felt a small flash of triumph that her words had cut him. He had no idea of the truth of what had sent her away from him, but that mattered very little. It hadn't for a long time.

"Yes, you are willful, that is true. But you are also a savvy businesswoman. You wouldn't allow your livelihood and reputation to be damaged, especially if you could prevent it by doing exactly what you've done with so many other men before." He smiled, but like his laugh, there was nothing friendly about it. "You may be many things, but you are not a fool."

Cassandra hesitated. What he was saying sounded like . . . blackmail. But what could he hold over her head?

"You are right that I wouldn't threaten my business, but I don't see how denying you could cause damage to me at all." She cocked her head, her heart beating faster as she waited for him to explain.

"Your toys, my dear." He leaned closer with an ugly smile. "You must know they are the key to your undoing."

She laughed. "Please, I would wager most if not all of the most influential people in the *ton* know about my side business. Half of them indulge in my wares from time to time."

What she said was purely a bluff. In truth, a very select few knew the truth about her toys. Men who wanted her special creations most often requested them through those third parties. This protected both her and the gentlemen she serviced.

"Please!" he barked. "Give me a small bit of credit. *Some* may know what you really do, what you really *are*. More may even suspect that you do something unsavory on the side, but it is hardly an open secret."

Cassandra swallowed hard. He knew so much of what she had hidden all these years. She was too shocked to deny the truth of his words.

But he didn't seem to require her response, for he continued, "What if someone were to prove to some of these stuffy matrons who so adore your gowns that you were contributing to their husbands' torrid affairs with mistresses? What if a person was to send a version of one of your toys to them directly? Would they want you to design clothing for them . . . for their innocent daughters?"

Cassandra's lips parted in horror. She had always danced along a delicate edge by designing erotic toys for distinguished, and she thought discreet, clients. But they had added enormously to her wealth, in fact, that portion of what she did was a mainstay of her survival.

But the sewing also paid her bills. And it exposed her to clients for both her businesses, even as it fed her creative soul. If she lost one, she would surely lose the other.

"Are you willing to risk that I am wrong?" Nathan said with a tilt of his head. "Are you willing to take a chance that the matrons will forgive you when your sinful side activities are thrown in their faces?"

"You wouldn't do that," she whispered, thinking again of the young man who had lain with her on the grassy hillsides of his country home and laughed as they compared shapes in the clouds.

"You don't know me anymore, Cassandra," he murmured.

She stared at him. "No. I never did."

His mouth twisted faintly in an expression of pain, but then he turned away from her. "I will expect a decision from you, Cassandra. Very soon. I do hope it will be the right one."

Without waiting for a response, Nathan strode to the door and out into her hallway. Cassandra did not make a sound until she heard the butler close the front door behind him with a smart click, and even then she waited until she was certain Nathan's carriage had departed her circular drive.

Only then did she cross to the parlor door, shut it and rest her head against the cool wooden surface with a moan. She fisted her hands against the door and pounded a few times, she even stomped her foot in a childish display of utter frustration.

But then she shook her head, smoothed her gown around her hips and began to think. She needed help in dealing with her current circumstance, and luckily she already had a caller coming this afternoon who might be the perfect adviser.

Until that time, all she could do was return to her mountain of work and try to pretend that she couldn't still taste Nathan on her lips. Try to pretend she didn't *like* tasting him there after all these years.

★ ★ ★

Stephan Undercliffe had always been a handsome man, with a tall, lanky body rippled with coils of lean muscle, dark hair that was almost black, and brown eyes that almost matched his hair, especially when he was aroused. Cassandra had certainly enjoyed their time together when she had been his mistress for nearly a year.

Stephan had been a marvelous lover, skilled with his mouth, his hands, his cock, and his words. Her very first erotic toy had been for their personal pleasure, and he had been so taken with the design that he had convinced her that others would desire such a thing as well. He had invested in her secondary business and even assisted her in soliciting her first few clients.

Their physical affiliation had long since ended, and he had slowly become her friend and business adviser. He hadn't been her last lover, but he had been a favorite. In truth, he still was.

And yet, even now she recognized that no moment of passion she had ever shared with Stephan compared to that one angry kiss with Nathan a few hours before.

She was in trouble and she could only pray that Stephan could help—at least with her business woes. No one beyond herself could make her behave less foolishly when it came to Nathan and the lust he stirred in her.

"You seem distracted, Cass," Stephan drawled, as he slowly twirled a carved ivory dildo she had been designing for a client in his hands.

Cassandra pursed her lips as she watched him turn the

object around and around, as if it were a cigar or a pencil. "That's not a toy, you know," she said, her tone a bit harsher than she had intended.

He smiled and just the corner of one side of his mouth lifting slowly. "Yes, it is, sweet. Remember?"

He arched both eyebrows and Cassandra rolled her eyes. "You know what I mean. That isn't yours; you shouldn't be . . . *playing* with it."

Stephan stood up from where he was sprawled on her settee and moved toward her slowly. "Are you certain you wouldn't like to take me up on my offer to test all your designs?"

When he reached her, Cassandra snatched the toy from his hands and gave him a playful push. "I didn't ask you here for that. But I do have another topic that perhaps you *can* assist me with."

Stephan's smile faltered just a fraction before he shrugged and returned to his seat. "Pity that. So what is on your mind, Cass?"

She found herself stroking the toy in her hand and shoved it back into its drawer with a huff of breath. Stephan was a bad influence. "When I first began designing my toys, you and I talked about the potential risk to my reputation and my livelihood as a seamstress." She frowned. "And you were correct that as long as I was discreet, used trusted third-party contacts whenever I could, and chose my clientele wisely that I could continue my double life. But . . ."

Stephan straightened up. "But?"

She pursed her lips. There was no easy way to say this.

"What if someone knew about what I did and wanted to make my activities public? What if they wished to make my toys an issue with the upper-class women of the *ton*?"

Now it was Stephan who frowned, and the expression was so rare on his handsome face that Cassandra's heart stuttered. She wasn't going to like his answer and she knew it before he uttered one syllable.

"You have many powerful friends," he began. "There is Darby, who still speaks very highly of you. And the Earl of Rothschild has remained a patron of your little side business even since his marriage."

"Yes," Cassandra said softly. "Both of them have been very kind, even after we ended our affairs."

He nodded. "While I don't have the titles of the other two, I do have some influence and money. If someone began to make trouble for you, we could probably protect you in some ways, but . . ."

He broke off and Cassandra clenched her fists to muster up a bit of strength. "But? Please continue, Stephan. Let us have it all."

He cleared his throat uncomfortably. "But once enough people knew the truth about your second living, I cannot lie to you and tell you that it wouldn't damage you. I would wager that a good many women would stop coming to you, preaching loudly about your bad influence on their darling daughters. And the men who utilized your toys might stay away as well."

Cassandra swallowed. "Because the trick of such a delicate

business is discretion and there would be no discretion any-more. Too many people would be watching."

With a nod, Stephan continued, "If it caused a big enough scandal, the papers might even pick up the story."

Cassandra covered her eyes with her hands. "Which would spell the end of me. Yes. That is what I thought, but I suppose I held out hope that you would provide me with some magical solution."

Stephan got to his feet and crossed the room to her. Taking her hands lightly in his own, he stared down at her. "So this is not a hypothetical, then. Someone is truly threatening you? Who is it? I promise to have him killed by noon tomorrow. Or the very least, severely terrified."

Cassandra laughed at the gentle teasing in her friend's voice. No matter how he tried to lighten her mood, though, the facts remained the same. "I don't think murder is the answer, tempting as it may be. And he is not a man to be so easily terrified," she said, as she drew her hands away and paced to her window. Down below was a pretty garden she loved to tend herself when she wasn't overpowered by work. Even the budding evidence of eminent flowers on her rose-bushes couldn't make her feel better.

The garden, after all, was paid for by her gowns and toys, as were her servants, her food, her bills, and the money she sent home to her family. Her living was made by her own hand, and she had little to fall back on unless she returned to the life of a mistress. She hadn't hated that role. In fact, she had found great pleasure in her protectors.

But living by another's whim terrified her. Even her past lovers, who had been kind and good to her, were not immune to eventual boredom with what she had to offer. Once that happened, a mistress was at the mercy of the next gentleman who showed interest. And if she were shunned by good Society, that would make finding a quality protector all the more difficult.

No, she preferred her independent life. She preferred to take a lover because she wanted him, not because she needed what he could provide financially. The passion and pleasure were so much more real then.

"Who, Cassandra?" Stephan pressed. "Who would threaten you? You have been very careful about who knows your business. The few who do are rich men in no need of taking your money. And you have so many satisfied customers that I doubt any of them would threaten their own pleasure by exposing your identity."

"He is not a customer." She scowled. "And his price is vengeance; it has nothing to do with money. It is a man who believes I wronged him in a personal matter. A matter of the heart."

Stephan's eyes widened. "Ah, well, that kind of blackmail tends to be the most insidious because there is rarely satisfaction on either side in the end. What can I do?"

Cassandra looked at him, truly seeing him again for the first time since they began their conversation. As he had said, he did not have the influence of some of her other lovers, but she was no longer close enough to any of those men to ask for their help. Even if she did, what could they do? There was no escaping Nathan's demand, no bartering for something other than what he wanted.

He wouldn't be satisfied until she was in his bed—controlled by him, surrendered to him sexually, physically and emotionally. She shivered and, to her dismay, it wasn't a shiver of distaste. Damn him and damn herself.

"There is nothing that can be done," she said softly, "except what I can do myself. But I do appreciate your hearing my plight and offering your assistance. Just your ear was enough."

She patted him on the cheek and he caught her hand, holding it gently against the rough stubble that was beginning to form there in the late hours of the afternoon. "I could at least help you ease the tension."

Cassandra smiled, even though there was an earnestness to his expression that made her heart ache. She had often suspected that Stephan might want her again, but now it was clear. And despite the fact that he was too damned attractive for his own good, she didn't want him. Their friendship meant too much to threaten.

And there was another man who filled her mind with wanton desires. It wouldn't be fair.

"No, Stephan. Though I am tempted by your offer, I don't think so." She gently extracted her hand from his cheek.

With a shrug, he said, "Well, if you won't allow me to reduce the strain, I hope you'll find some other way. If you feel you must face this unnamed man alone, you will want to do it with as much calm as possible. And right now you are wound so tightly that I could strum you like a lute string."

Cassandra nodded as she walked him to the door. "Perhaps you are correct. Though I'm not certain how to do that at present."

He smiled as he paused in the foyer. "Of course you do, my dear. You make toys. Go play."

Chapter Three

Cassandra stood in her bedroom, staring at the open chest of drawers beside her big four-poster bed. The chamber sparkled from a dozen lit candles and the roaring fire her servants had prepared to heat the room.

As a designer of sinful toys for the rich and titled, Cassandra had spent a great deal of time testing out the merits of each design. It was an enormously pleasurable pursuit, one that had given a few of her lovers as much excitement as it had her.

But she had been increasingly busy as of late. No man had been in her bed for half a year, perhaps a little more. The sheer night shifts and sinful undergarments she had designed hung unworn in her armoire, while some of her favorite toys in her drawer had been ignored for a long while. Restraints wrapped in soft fur, little clips to tighten and arouse her nipples or her clit, blindfolds to heighten sensation and awareness—all of them had been sadly unused.

Only one toy had come out of the drawer with any regularity. A glass dildo similar in size to the ivory one she had been working on downstairs. It was her own personal plaything.

Stephan said she was coursing with tension. And he was correct that she better face Nathan when she was relaxed and satiated. Perhaps then his presence wouldn't make her wet and ready, as weak physically as her mind seemed to be when it came to him.

She grasped the long, heavy weight of the toy and withdrew it, then shrugged from her silken robe. Freshly bathed, she was warm and ready for pleasure after such a trying day.

Resting back on her pillows, she opened her legs and began to stroke the glass head of the substitute cock along the swollen lips of her sex. Her body had experienced this pleasure enough times that it began to react almost immediately. She shut her eyes and enjoyed the pulse of desire as her outer lips swelled and her pussy grew hot and wet in readiness.

Smiling, Cassandra felt her body relax, open, flush with excitement. This was the gift she gave her clients. She wasn't ashamed of helping to enhance their pleasure. And she wasn't ashamed of wanting and needing her own. She had let go of shame a long time ago.

Slowly, she let the head of the cool glass rod slip inside her waiting body. Instantly, her body tightened around the surface, clinging when she gently teased the shaft away. She delved deeper the next time, then withdrew a second time. Again and again, she repeated the shallow strokes until finally the toy was fully seated in her channel and she pulsed in pleasure around its rapidly heating surface.

Cassandra understood her own desire. She knew how to bring herself to swift and satisfying release. Immediately she thrust with the motion and speed that always brought her to orgasm quickly. The wet slap of the glass as she fucked herself and her low moans of pleasure were the only sounds in her quiet room. She arched her hips against the building pressure, reaching higher and higher for release.

Just as she neared the pinnacle, the image of Nathan's face entered her mind. She cried out, recalling the feel of his arms crushing her to his chest, the scent of his skin. She could almost taste his mouth, feel the hard thrust of his aroused cock through his trousers as he ground against her.

Her orgasm was powerful, the strongest she had experienced in quite some time. She thrashed on the bed, her eyes squeezed shut, trying not to lose the erotic images of Nathan, even though she hated herself for using his blackmail—his demands—to find her pleasure.

Finally, the quaking tremors of her wet body subsided. She shivered one last time around the glass cock in her hand and then withdrew it with a soft pop.

She set the toy aside and flopped a forearm over her eyes as her heart rate slowed to a normal rhythm and her breath became deeper and less erratic. Although she was warm and flushed with pleasure now, allowing herself release through her toy hadn't done what she desired.

She had hoped that bringing herself to orgasm would release the tension that Nathan's demands . . . no, not just his demands, the man himself had created. Instead, she now felt more tightly wound than ever. Pleasure had turned to fantasy. And soon, no matter how much she tried to pretend she didn't want it to happen, fantasy would become reality.

As she drifted off into fitful, erotically charged sleep, she mused on how she couldn't wait for that moment.

Nathan stood in Cassandra's parlor. It was not the one he had intruded upon the previous day, the room she had converted into a studio for her work, but a different place. He gazed around with a frown. He preferred the cluttered disarray of her workroom, where her personality and passion invaded every corner. This chamber revealed *nothing* about Cassandra's life. It was plain and pretty and it looked like any other parlor in any other rich person's home in London.

But Cassandra wasn't like anyone else. She was tempting and frustrating. She was a seductress, a liar, not to be trusted. He couldn't forget that, no matter how much this unwanted, driving, angry need to touch her overwhelmed him.

She was the enemy.

The door to the room opened and Cassandra stepped inside. As she quietly closed the door behind her, Nathan straightened up and stared at her. When he last saw her all those years ago, her red hair had been tangled down around her shoulders, she had been wearing a half-unbuttoned gown, well made by her tailor father, but not fancy. She had been laughing and making false promises about meeting him that night, running away with him to Gretna Green.

She had looked like exactly what she was, an upper middle class daughter of a man in trade.

Today she looked like a queen. Her green gown was the finest silk money could buy, draped perfectly over her form in what would surely be the grandest style of the Season. The cut of her bodice accentuated her full breasts, despite the fact that a more boyish figure was the current rage. And her hair was bound up in a complicated, layered and curled arrangement on the top of her head. Something that would require at least one servant to assist in creating.

Her clothing and her hair and everything about the way she held herself said that she was a lady of quality. A lie. But a well-told one.

"Good morning," Cassandra said, intruding upon his reverie with a thin-lipped, humorless smile. "I did not expect you to return to my home so soon."

"Hoping for a reprieve?" he asked. "That I might forget about yesterday's conversation?"

She sighed. "If you did not forget about me during the four years we have been apart, I think it would be foolish to hope you would forget me in the span of less than twenty-four hours, especially when you are so determined to follow through with your plans."

He turned away, hating how he had made his obsession with her so clear. His angry kiss had told her as plain as words that he had spent some part of every day while he was away from England thinking of her. Dreaming of her. Hating her and the fact that she had convinced him that she loved him.

She who loved no one but herself.

"Why should I stay away?" he asked, as he looked out the window at her small but tidy garden. "Why should I make this more comfortable for you?"

"No reason," she said, and her voice was brittle enough that he turned. "No reason at all. Let us set the terms of this . . . arrangement then, shall we?"

His lips parted. Her hands were clenched behind her back and she looked for all the world like she was marching toward the guillotine rather than his bed, but the fact remained that she didn't appear to be preparing to fight him.

"You are agreeing to my demands?" he asked, almost in disbelief. He had actually been looking forward to doing battle with her today. Her sudden surrender was unexpected.

She shrugged delicately. "It seems I have little choice. You are determined to ruin me if I do not bend to your will, and though I have doubts that you won't simply destroy me even when this bargain has ended, this is my only option. I must do as you ask and pray you are a man of your word."

Nathan's cheek twitched. "*You* are daring to question my word?"

Fire flashed in her eyes for the first time since she entered the chamber. "*You* are the one making threats, Nathan."

He crossed the room in three long strides and caught her upper arms in his grip. He yanked her against him with little gentleness. "I was never the liar between the two of us, Cassandra. I showed up that night," he hissed.

She stared at him for a long moment, searching his eyes, his very soul. Then she shook her head with what seemed to be a combination of sadness and disdain. "Tell me what your terms are, Nathan. Let us just finish this."

He released her and paced a few steps away. "I told you. You will come to my bed, for as long as I desire you to be there. I expect I'll bore of you soon enough."

"I expect so," she said without expression or inflection.

He arched a brow, driven to hurt her now. "Besides, I am here in London to find a wife. Once I have found her, I will be a *faithful* husband and I won't need a mistress any longer."

She nodded once. "Very well. Then you expect our affiliation will not last out the Season?"

He examined her face carefully. She had added no special emphasis to her words and her maddeningly cool expression had not changed, yet there was a faint look of sadness in her eyes. He stared at the flicker, shocked by the fact that it shamed him to know he had put it there.

Didn't she deserve that much? Christ, after she broke her vow and he left the country, he had spent much of a year drinking and feeling sorry for himself. Didn't he owe her some fraction of that pain in return?

He looked away so he could no longer see her quietly accusing eyes. "I assume a Season is all it will take."

He shrugged. He wasn't being arrogant in that assumption. Already he was somewhat of an attention getter when he paid calls with his mother. With his money and his appearance, he was certain he would have his pick of women.

"And what is my guarantee that once you have tired of my body, you won't simply turn around and betray me?" she asked. "You say your word is the promise you can give me, but is that all you can offer as proof?"

He did look at her then. And again he was brought back to what he thought her to be when he fell in love with her and asked her to be his bride, Society and his father be damned.

How fine she had been then. As smart as any person he had ever met, with a sharp tongue to boot. Obviously, those things hadn't changed about her. She still had the light of intelligence and strength in her eyes. But when he met her, she was devoid of any pretense or greed . . . or so he thought. She had been so different from any other woman he'd ever met that he couldn't help but be captivated by her.

A fact made more powerful by how innocent she had seemed. How pretty she was.

Now, she was different. She had certainly grown in beauty, coming into her looks with the certainty of a woman. But Cassandra had also become jaded. And why not? Certainly she had lied and double-crossed to get what she wanted. Her success in business proved that, her long string of former lovers proved it further.

Why wouldn't she hold him to the same low standard?

"My word is my bond," he said in a low voice. "You will have to trust it. As you say, you have little choice."

She nodded once, the motion jerky and short. "Very well, I agree, however reluctantly. But you must realize that while I may surrender to your whims in order to save myself, I don't promise to make any attempt to sooth your ego."

He chuckled at that. Before he asked her to be his wife, they had been engaged in an intensely sexual affair. She had been young and inexperienced at the time, but he had pleased her. And he had never had any complaints from any other woman who warmed his bed in the interim. Of his prowess, he was very secure.

"So, you are saying you won't pretend pleasure just to keep me happy?" he said as he moved toward her a few slow steps at a time.

Her eyes widened, but she stayed in her place, even when he threaded his fingers into her hair and began to massage her scalp. The complicated hairstyle that proved she was a lady fell around her shoulders in thick, auburn waves.

"It's a very good thing that I won't make you pretend, then," he said softly, as his lips descended. "All your pleasure will be quite real, I assure you."

She pulled back then, straining against the hold of his fingers. "What are you doing?" she asked, but her breath was short.

"There is no time like the present to begin the inevitable, my dear."

Before she could protest, he smashed his lips to hers. He meant the kiss to be punishing and dominating, but that didn't last for long. As soon as he tasted her, his body relaxed, his mouth grew less harsh, and he allowed himself to revel in the kiss.

In so many ways she was deceptively the same—so sweet, so warm, so fresh. And she was his, even if it was only to save her own hide.

She fought to retain her distance, he felt it in her thin lips and in the way she kept her neck stiff, even as he lightly massaged the tense muscle there. But slowly, as he licked and nibbled along the break in her lips, her barriers began to erode until finally she parted her mouth and sucked his tongue inside with a needy hunger that matched the fervor of his own.

They clawed at each other, finding fastenings and hooks as the kiss spiraled completely out of control. When he felt the delicate silk of her gown rend at a seam, he didn't even pause, he just slid his hungry mouth over to the bare skin he had revealed at her shoulder.

She hissed in a breath, rolling and arching her hips against his in a harsh, circular motion. Her body stroked his cock so perfectly he felt like he could spend right then and there, but he wasn't going to give her the satisfaction of taking what he was not ready to give.

He responded by spinning her around and cradling her backside against his hips as he glided his hand down the back of her gown, his fingers popping the line of buttons there with practiced skill.

She arched as her dress fell forward, revealing the most sinfully sheer chemise he had ever seen.

Cassandra smiled when all of Nathan's movements ceased. Ah, so he appreciated the erotic undergarment she had designed. It hadn't been worn for some time, so she was glad its effect was as potent as ever. Reveling in the power such a simple thing could wield, she took advantage of his suddenly loosened grip and turned around, as she dropped her fine gown away.

The chemise was fitted just right—loose enough to skim suggestively over her skin, but tight enough that the transparent fabric revealed the swollen pink tips of her nipples and the shadow where her thighs met.

When she had put the undergarment on that morning, she had pretended it wasn't for Nathan's benefit. But now, as he stared, mouth slightly agape, she recognized what a foolish lie that had been. She had known exactly what would happen.

This garment was a way to retain power, to prove to him and to herself that she could steal his control and make him tremble.

"Very nice," he finally murmured with a hard swallow, "as pretty as I remember you being."

Without any further comment, he reached out and grasped the filmy fabric. With a downward jerking motion, he rended it in half, leaving the loose ends to flutter uselessly around her hips.

So much for power and control.

He looked her up and down as she pushed the torn fabric away. "Yes, very pretty, indeed."

Then his body was against hers again. She had only managed to remove his overcoat in her haste and open a few of his shirt buttons. So she was naked while he remained fully clothed. When she reached up to remedy that discrepancy, he caught her hands and pulled them behind her back gently.

She hesitated as his lips found her throat and he began to swirl wicked patterns against her sensitive skin with his tongue. So this was his intent. To have her without even revealing himself to her. To not bother undressing since he had no intention of staying once he spent his lust and anger.

She didn't fight when he spun her around so that her bare backside fit against his hips a second time. Through the woolen fabric of his trousers she felt the insistent, heavy length of his cock. He had been her first lover and her biggest one, as well. She shivered when she recalled all the masterful things he could do with that cock.

Her own words taunted her as he bent her over the settee and she felt his fingers slip between their bodies to loosen his trouser fastenings. She had said she wouldn't pretend pleasure for his benefit, but there wasn't going to be any pretending. Wet, sticky heat already betrayed her as it trickled down her inner thighs. Her nipples were sensitive as they rasped against the soft upholstered fabric of the settee, and she tensed when she felt the hot, thick head of his cock glide back and forth against her waiting opening.

But she clung to the idea that as much as he could play her body like a violin, even after all these years, she could do the same to him. So she thrust back, forcing his erection into her body.

Nathan's fingers tightened against Cassandra's hips, tight enough that he realized she might be bruised tomorrow. He had been teasing rather than taking for the simple reason that he thought he might lose all control the moment he entered her hot, tight sheath. Perhaps she had sensed that, perhaps she had wanted to unman him with a few heavenly squeezes of her slick inner walls.

But maybe her intent was far less Machiavellian. Perhaps she merely wanted him with the same desperation that churned in his gut. Perhaps she just couldn't wait to feel him buried inside of her.

Either way, he thrust forward and let the final few inches of his cock slip deeply into her. Her back arched when his hips bumped the luscious curve of her backside. He shut his eyes and took a brief moment to wonder at the fact that being inside of her was as good as all his dreams.

It was better.

Then he shut his thoughts away and began to fuck her. Not make love to her, not take his time, he couldn't do those things. No, he just wanted to feel the slide and pull of pounding in and out of her clenching channel.

Their skin slapped together as he slammed his body into hers, but he didn't hear her complaining. In fact, she had long since stopped making coherent words and moved into a mixture of gasps, moans, and a few choice curses that he rarely heard women use.

She grew flushed and then her nails dug into the settee, her back arched, and she let out a cry that all but shook the room. Her pussy clenched so tight around him that he let out his own cry of pure pleasure. His seed began to move, his legs began to shake, and he pulled his cock from her body to milk the proof of his pleasure onto her skin rather than inside of her.

The room was silent for a moment that seemed to stretch forever. Then Cassandra stood from her splayed position bent over the little couch and turned toward him. She looked every inch the queen, nothing like the whore he had just treated her like.

"There, the bargain is sealed," she said softly. She would have sounded unaffected, too, if not for the fact that her breath was still short and her skin still flushed from her powerful orgasm.

"It is," he said as he buttoned his trousers and snatched up his jacket from the floor. It was tangled with her gown and he frowned as he shook the silky fabric away.

"When will you return?" she asked, gathering her own things and holding them in front of her naked body like a cloth shield.

He shrugged. "When I want you, I will be back. Be ready."

Her eyes narrowed and he could see how much she wanted to bite out what would no doubt be a scathing set down, but she bit her lip and instead executed a curt nod.

"As you wish, Lord Blackhearth."

Nathan winced. She hadn't called him by his full title since the day they met, and that was too many years ago to count. It put an undeniable wall between them, higher than even his anger or his dismissive use of her body.

He shrugged. It didn't matter. He had what he'd come for, after all. Let her stew.

"Good day, Miss Willows," he said, as he swung the parlor door open and left her home.

It wasn't until he settled into his plush carriage that he realized he had found his own pleasure only after she reached the height of hers. And that it had been his most powerful sexual experience in recent memory.

Chapter Four

_I_ hear you saw Cassandra Willows."

Nathan almost choked on his mouthful of venison. He coughed, covering his mouth, as he stared down the long dining table at his father.

The Marquis of Herstale was no longer the man of Nathan's youth. He recalled his father as big, strapping, and capable of anything and everything. But two years of illness that culminated in near death just a few months before had stolen much from the man. Now he was a shadow of himself.

But as for power, the Marquis still had that, just not the physical kind. Nathan didn't doubt the man had spies and confidantes all over London. Ones who had been watching _him_, apparently. And from the sounds of things, they knew of his wicked visit to Cassandra the previous morning. How much more had they uncovered?

When Nathan could breathe again he took a bracing sip of red wine and said, "Where did you hear that?"

It wasn't a direct denial; it wasn't really an answer at all, but until he discovered what his father actually knew, he had no intention of accidentally revealing something.

"From me, dear heart," his mother said from the other end of the table. "I was with you when we encountered *that woman* at your Aunt Worthington's, remember?"

Relief massaged the tension from Nathan's shoulders. Ah, yes, he'd all but forgotten the fact that his mother had been present that first, charged moment when he heard Cassandra's voice and saw her face. They had not spoken of the encounter afterward, probably because his sisters were in the vehicle with them, and the two girls were far too young to recall the bitter past their family shared with the seamstress.

"That is why we wished to see you without your siblings present," his father said, confirming what Nathan had already guessed. "This situation . . ."

Nathan interrupted with a wave of his hand. "Come now, that little moment at Aunt Bethany's could hardly be called a 'situation.'" Blackmailing Cassandra into being his sex slave could be, but what his parents didn't know wouldn't hurt them.

His mother shook her head. "I saw your face after she left, Nathan. An accidental encounter might not be a situation, but your expression was, my dear." She hesitated and her eyes were soft and kind. "Do you think yourself still in love with that girl?"

Nathan's stomach tensed. Love. That was something he didn't think much about. Since Cassandra had thrown him over, he didn't believe he'd ever feel love again. Even now, the best he hoped for was to find a match with woman who was attractive to him, one he liked well enough to look at across the breakfast table every morning for the rest of his life. Someone who could provide him with children to carry on his family legacy.

Love was an entirely different weakness that he didn't intend to explore ever again. Certainly not with Cassandra. He wouldn't allow that to happen under any circumstances. For her, he would allow desire, of course. Anger, yes.

Nothing more.

"Philippa!" his father barked from his end of the table. "Let us not speak of such things."

Nathan frowned. His father had been vocal about his disapproval of Nathan's match with Cassandra all those years ago. It had caused a rift between them at the time that had grown ever wider when Nathan realized his father was right and she didn't love him as she claimed. Apparently, thoughts of that troubled time still stung, because Arthur Manning was shifting in his chair uncomfortably.

Nathan raised a hand. "I will not deny that seeing Cassandra—Miss Willows—for the first time after all these years was quite a surprise, but it was bound to happen. After all, she is a popular dressmaker amongst our circles. Now that the shock is over, I have everything under control. You two needn't worry yourselves over her."

He smiled in reassurance at both his parents, even as a niggling little voice from deep inside reminded him that he could hardly be called "under control" when it came to Cassandra. But ultimately, his blackmail would allow him to purge this ridiculous desire he had to feel her body under his, around his, riding his.

And then it *would* be over. On his terms this time.

His mother's brow wrinkled slightly, as if she weren't as sure of his statement as he pretended to be. But his father nodded with a grunt.

"Damn right," the Marquis said, as he fidgeted with the stem of his wineglass. He didn't look at Nathan. "You would be a damn fool to mix yourself up with that woman again. And love, Philippa, really! As if Nathan would ever love a woman who made a fool of him that way. Our son is far more intelligent than all that."

Nathan felt his smile beginning to fall a fraction as his father spoke.

"He might have been lovesick once, but he learned his lesson. That woman can't be trusted. She was a whore and she's in trade, for God's sake!"

His mother winced slightly at the blunt terms. "But she did choose that over ruining our son, so I suppose we must give her credit for finally recognizing her true station in life. She could have destroyed Nathan's future entirely if she had shown up at their rendezvous."

Nathan shut his eyes as images bombarded him: Standing in the dark behind the village inn at midnight, his heart so full of love, his future so sure in his mind. Still standing there at one. At two. At three when the rain had begun to pour. It had been a cold, gray dawn before he finally stopped being an ass and returned home.

And there had been his father, awaiting his return, with a note he had somehow intercepted between Cassandra and another man. Her own words, ones she hadn't ever intended him to see, had explained everything in blunt detail. They had shattered Nathan's soul.

He opened his eyes with a growl of displeasure. He had stopped reliving that moment years ago, he wasn't about to indulge in such maudlin activities again.

He pushed to his feet. "We all know what happened," he snapped, as he tossed his napkin onto his half-eaten food. "There is no use discussing it. You don't have to worry about Cassandra. Rest assured, there is no way I would ever let her into my heart to manipulate me again. Now if you will excuse me, this is not a topic I wish to discuss."

His mother opened her mouth to respond, but Nathan silenced her with a brief kiss on the forehead before he exited the dining room and the house.

All these reminders of what had happened in the past only served to feed the anger and resentment that still boiled in his chest. And there was only one person who deserved those bitter emotions.

So it was time to pay her another visit.

Cassandra sat on the high, cushioned stool and leaned over her worktable as she focused on stitching a fur lining onto a special pair of restraints. With everything that had been going on in her life the last few days, she was behind on her work, both as a seamstress and for her side business.

Damn Nathan for both those things. And now that she had no idea when he might barge into her life or summon her to demand sexual favors, she had to work doubly hard when he wasn't around just to be certain she finished everything she was obliged to create. The last thing she needed was to fall behind and lose face with her customers. Some of them were very unforgiving.

Just like Nathan. She sighed as she straightened up. After all this time, he still hated her. Enough that he might very well destroy her. And yet the hot desire that had always existed between them remained. It had certainly given a harsh edge to the sex between them the day before. She had never made love to a man who could hardly stand her before. With a shiver, she tried to forget the rough slide of Nathan's cock inside of her and refocus instead on the restraints.

The door opened behind her and she turned. Her butler stood in the doorway, his face a mask of upset. "*He* has returned, Miss Willows," the man said without preamble.

The item in her hand clattered down onto the worktable and Cassandra stifled a curse. There was no need to explain who "he" was. It was abundantly clear. "Let him come in," she said. There was no denying him.

The servant opened the door, but before he could move, Nathan pushed past him into her work area for the second time in a week.

"Tell him that when I come, I am allowed to see you, no matter where you are," he ordered without even acknowledging that the servant remained in the room.

Cassandra pushed to her feet and stared at him evenly while the heat of embarrassment flooded her cheeks. She rather liked her servants and hated to have them see her in such a dominated position.

"Tell him," Nathan repeated.

She set her jaw as she said, "Wilkes, whenever Lord Blackhearth comes to call, please make sure he is sent to me directly. He does not need announcement or permission."

The butler's eyes went wide at the order, but then he bowed his acknowledgment. "Yes, Miss Willows. Will you need anything else tonight?"

She shook her head. "It is late. You may retire, as may the other servants. Good night."

Her servant cast a second glance at Nathan, but then he left the room.

"There is no need to be cruel," Cassandra said softly, as she moved passed Nathan and closed the door that Wilkes had left open out of some kind of desire to protect her. As if he could. "I am giving you what you want."

When she turned around, she jumped in surprise. Nathan had her crowded up against the door and was now less than an inch away. He bracketed his hands against the surface behind her and leaned in so that his hot breath stirred her hair.

"Cruel?" he murmured, as his lips brushed the delicate, sensitive skin behind her ear.

Cassandra sucked in a breath as pleasure arced from the point of contact and hardened her nipples in an instant. Clearly, Nathan remembered a great deal about how to arouse her. Long ago he had teased her, saying he would keep her in line with just kisses against her neck. Now, that seemed prophetic rather than amusing.

"You have no idea of cruelty," he said, as he grasped her earlobe between his teeth and tugged ever so gently.

She arched, hating her body for betraying his effect on her. And wanting more of him. More of everything.

He pushed away from her, as if he sensed her desire and was determined to deny her for a little while. He paced away and looked around the room. He froze when his gaze settled on her worktable.

Cassandra had never been ashamed of her side business. She protected it, but not because she thought it was wrong. She just knew the consequences if talk of her toys became too loud.

But the way Nathan's mouth twisted in disapproval made

her gaze flit away from him and more heat flood her cheeks. His eyes narrowed as he stared at the items she had created: the half-finished restraints, the open lockbox on the table that held a few dildos, a scrap of fabric that was on its way to being a scandalous piece of lingerie. They were the tools of lusty men bent on having their every desire.

A bit like the one before her.

"Working late, eh?" he asked, lifting the restraints and turning to dangle them on one finger in her direction.

She pursed her lips. "I have no choice. Since you insist that I be available to you at your discretion, I must use whatever time I do have to myself to fulfill my obligations. These people have paid me a great deal of money in exchange for their goods. It would be wrong of me to renege on my promise to deliver."

"How nice that you keep your word for money. Perhaps if I had only paid you, you would have shown up all those years ago," he said, his voice chilly. "Do you have a pair of these that are finished?"

Cassandra couldn't help raising her brows in surprise. Then she smoothed the reaction from her face. He wanted to shock and embarrass her. There was little she could do to prevent him from taking what he desired, but at least she could deny him this one satisfaction.

"Yes, upstairs."

Now his brows lifted. "Your own personal collection?"

She nodded, the motion difficult in the face of his intense scrutiny. "Yes."

"Lead the way," he said, motioning his hand toward the

door with false gallantry. "I want to see the toy box of the master toy maker herself."

Cassandra narrowed her eyes at his sarcasm, but said nothing. Instead, she turned and opened the parlor door, leading the way to her chamber upstairs in anything but companionable silence. Before she pushed the door open, she drew a deep breath.

This room was her sanctuary, her private escape. There was no denying Nathan access, but once he had been inside, she knew she would never see the room the same way again. He would burn his presence into every inch of space until he stifled her.

But she had no choice. She had to let him in . . . in every way, or suffer the consequences.

So she opened the door and motioned for him to enter.

Chapter Five

Cassandra shut the bedroom door, letting her head rest against the cool surface for a long moment as she gathered her wavering nerves. Finally, she pivoted and watched Nathan move around her room. He seemed as aware of his effect on her space as she was, and took his time looking at her furniture, examining her subdued artwork, and glancing out her window toward her garden in the dark below.

"Not what I pictured," he said, turning back to her. "I assumed a woman with your checkered past would have much more blatant taste. Is there some other chamber where you entertained your protectors?"

She frowned, anger and hurt bubbling up in her chest. "So many insults, I can scarce keep up with them all. What has put you in such a foul mood, Nathan?"

He seemed surprised by her direct question and shook his head in response. "I was simply reminded of the past tonight, reminded of what a fool I was. I am always in a foul mood after that."

She nodded slowly. "And just who reminded you?"

He locked eyes with her. "My parents. My father."

Cassandra couldn't help but stiffen as she thought of the Marquis of Herstale. He had hated her from the moment he realized she was more to his son than merely a brief affair. The man had done everything in his power to separate them. And he had won in the end, at a hefty cost to everyone involved.

"I see," she said softly. "And so you came here tonight to punish me?"

Again, Nathan's gaze swung to her and he stared at her for a long moment, as if he hadn't truly seen her until that moment. He opened his mouth and shut it a few times before he whispered, "I don't know, Cassandra. I truly do not know."

She wanted to turn away, but it was impossible when she could finally see a glimpse of the man she had once known. When she could read Nathan's emotions and, for the first time, they didn't only consist of lust and hatred. There was sadness there. Regret.

She realized she was moving toward him, although she hadn't meant to do so. He stiffened as she reached up and traced his lips with a finger, then his jaw. But he didn't resist when she lifted to her tiptoes and gently pressed her lips to his.

They kissed for what could have been an hour or it might

have only been a moment, Cassandra wasn't certain. Time lost all meaning when she was in Nathan's arms, it always had. These kisses weren't the angry demands he had issued before, and they weren't lusty promises, even though the taste of him did arouse her.

No, these kisses were gentle, soft explorations. The reunion they hadn't allowed for, even though their bodies had joined. The remembrance of a past that had been filled with so much love and laughter before it was cut short.

She melted against his chest, wrapping her arms around his neck, and clinging as their lips brushed and teased, tasted and retreated with a sweetness that almost brought tears to her eyes.

But then Nathan stiffened. She felt him push her away with his spirit and his heart just a fraction of a moment before he extracted himself from her arms physically.

"Don't try to manipulate me," he said, his breath short and rough with fresh anger. "I am immune to you now."

Cassandra stared at him, her own anger and frustration overtaking reason and restraint. "If you are so immune, why are you here? Why are you blackmailing me for something as intimate as sex if you truly cannot stand the sight of me?"

Nathan folded his arms and glared at her, but didn't gift her with the courtesy of a response.

She threw up her hands as she crossed the room to the chest beside her bed. "What is it that you want, Nathan? What do you have to gain?" She pulled a drawer away from the chest and dumped it unceremoniously on her bed. Toys and restraints scattered across her coverlet. "Are these what you want to see?"

He stared at her as she made her way to the armoire and pulled it wide open, yanking down a few of her more revealing undergarments.

"These?" She turned on him and held them up before she tossed them in his direction. "Here they are. And I am yours, that is the bargain we made." She unfastened the dainty buttons along the front of her gown and let the silky fabric fall away. "So do what you will."

Nathan frowned, as if her surrender was less pleasing to him than he thought it would be, but then he shook the reaction away and stalked toward her bed. He grasped up her restraints, a prettier, more elaborate version of the ones she had been making downstairs. Without preamble, he swept the remaining toys away, leaving them to clatter on the floor and fall to the table beside the bed.

"Take off the chemise," he ordered as he moved toward her.

She did as she had been told, but not in the way she had been told to do it. Unlike his barked order that implied swift, efficient action, she took her time removing the last swish of fabric that separated him from total access.

Little by little, she glided the thin strap down one shoulder, never revealing more than a little bit of skin. Then she moved to the opposite side, gliding it away just as slowly and deliberately.

When the straps had been removed, only the full curve of her breasts held the chemise in place. Nathan had stopped moving and was staring at her, his eyes glazed with heated interest. She couldn't help but smile as she tugged ever so gently on the fabric covering her breasts. It slipped a fraction of an inch, revealing more of the swell, but not quite everything.

Nathan caught his breath as the fabric moved even lower, just enough that the top half of her areolas were revealed.

"Enough, Cassandra," he murmured, his voice rough with desire. "Take it off."

Again, she smiled, enjoying the game between them, perhaps for the first time. As a young woman, she had been too inexperienced to toy with him, to utilize her feminine powers to their fullest. But now, with several lovers and a fuller understanding of sex as her guide, Cassandra *liked* knowing that as much as their current affair was a punishment and a blackmail, she could still control Nathan on some level.

She could still make him desire her like there was no other woman in the world.

With another pull, she let the chemise fold over her waist and revealed her breasts. Nathan growled low in his chest and triumph puffed her up.

"All of it," he ordered, but he wasn't moving to force her hand. He clenched the soft restraints in a death grip, but never overpowered her.

She shimmied and let the chemise glide down slowly, until it pooled around her feet with her discarded gown. He sucked in a breath, and suddenly Cassandra was glad she had left her fancy, handstitched red stockings and high heeled slippers on, rather than slip them off for comfort as she worked.

"You are more beautiful than . . ." he began, then cut himself off, as if he wouldn't allow himself to compliment her even in the smallest way. He lifted the restraints. "Come over here."

She moved toward him with a slow, purposeful swish of her hips. "You can fasten those to my bed," she said, as she reached him.

His eyes widened as he looked at the bedposts. She had installed small hooks on each one during her time with one lover who liked to use and have restraints used on him. She'd never removed them.

"Lie down," he said, and his voice was laced with frustration as well as lust.

She didn't argue, but took a place in the middle of her big bed, perfectly positioned for the velvety restraints that dangled from his big hands. Her heart fluttered like hummingbird wings in her chest as she stared up at him, waiting for him to tie her down. She would be at his mercy then and, at the moment, he didn't seem particularly merciful.

But never did she think he would hurt her. That was the strangest part. He could easily physically harm her, especially once she was bound and unable to defend herself, but even in the height of his anger, she knew his weapons would be pleasure, not pain.

He cupped her hand with his much larger one, the rough slide of his skin eliciting a soft groan that she couldn't withhold. She thought she saw the fleeting shadow of a smile cross his lips before he slipped the soft binding around her wrist.

He looped the other end over the hook on her bedpost and then tightened the fabric until she couldn't move her arm more than a few inches one way or the other.

He did the same with both her ankles and then her opposite wrist, taking his time to bind her, gentle in the way he tightened the restraints. Once she was fully at his mercy, he backed away, watching her through a hooded, unreadable gaze.

A wash of panic rushed through Cassandra as an unbidden thought pierced her haze.

"You aren't going to leave me like this, are you?" she whispered. Though her servants were discreet, it still wasn't a humiliation she desired.

He jerked back in surprise, then tilted his head as if he were now considering the merits of such an action. Finally, he shook his head. "As tempting as that might be, I want you more than I wish to leave you exposed and disgraced." He sighed, as if maligning his own weakness.

Cassandra relaxed a fraction at his reassurance, but it was a fleeting reprieve from tension. The moment Nathan's hands trailed to his waist and he began to unfasten his trousers, she stiffened.

When they had sex in her parlor the previous afternoon, she hadn't been able to see him. He had kept his body from her, she supposed as some kind of message. But now his fingers worked deftly at divesting himself of his jacket, his crisply tailored vest and shirt, and his fitted trousers. She stared in wonder at the slow revealing of taut, tanned flesh and muscle. When he finally was fully naked before her, she couldn't help but lick her lips in approval.

She had dreamed of his body during their time apart. Even years later, she'd been able to conjure an easy image of his nude form, which always excited her. Sometimes just the thought of his nakedness made her come when she pleasured herself.

But this . . . this was better than memory. The years apart, when he had lived in a wild country with less strict codes of conduct, had been very kind to him. He was more muscular than she remembered, his skin tanned with a healthy glow like he was outside without protection on a regular basis. But there were parts of him that were as beautiful as ever. His cock, already at attention, curled up against his stomach— big and thick, and hard as granite.

She found herself straining against the bonds with a powerful desire to touch him, to see if his flesh was as warm as it appeared, to grip his erection in her palm and stroke it, to kiss the crook of his shoulder and the flat plain of his belly.

When he chuckled low in his chest, she stopped moving. *That* was part of why he had restrained her; he knew she would want to touch him. Yesterday he had not let her see, today she couldn't touch. At no point did he ever intend to allow her all of him, in body or soul.

And he wanted her to know that fact full-well.

But even as he kept her from touching him, the heated intensity of his stare let it be known that he had every intention of touching her. She shivered in anticipation as he joined her on the foot of the bed, kneeling at her ankles.

"I can do anything to you," he mused, cupping her calves with warm fingers and massaging ever so gently.

Cassandra couldn't help arching at the touch.

"Oh, Nathan," she groaned with great difficulty. "You could have done anything to me even without the restraints. You know that. Whatever else this blackmail is, it's evident we still want each other."

He cocked his head at her straightforward assessment of their current situation, but then he shrugged one muscular shoulder. "Perhaps, but I rather like seeing you at my mercy. Unable to respond. Unable to spin your web of seduction around me. Unable to squirm away . . . or closer . . . when I do this. . . ."

He leaned down and pressed his lips to the smooth curve of her knee. Cassandra shut her eyes with a hiss of expelled breath as the pleasure of his touch ricocheted through her.

"Or this . . ." His mouth moved higher, his tongue teasing her inner thigh.

His mouth was almost unbearably hot against her ultrasensitive skin. He swirled his tongue around and around, alternating between licking and then blowing the damp swirls with heated breath. Slowly, he nibbled and tasted his way higher and higher until his hair began to tickle the wet outer lips of her pussy.

Her back arched and she tugged against the restraints help-lessly. How she wanted to tangle her fingers in his short, crisp hair, to cup his cheek as he pleasured her. To demand that he kiss her—and where.

Instead, all she could do was moan helplessly when he ex-pelled a sigh against the juncture of her thighs. The steamy breath seemed to penetrate her aching, clenching channel and fill her. She bit her lip to hold back a cry of intense, unex-pected pleasure.

Nathan lifted his eyes and met her gaze. His bright blue eyes were totally focused on her, a wicked, tempting glint in them that told her he knew exactly what kind of torment he was inflicting.

It told her that he had only just begun.

She couldn't help but smile down at him, ready to be swept away by a long night of teasing and torment, of plea-sure given and taken. It didn't matter why he was with her, only that he was there.

He lowered his attention back to her already soaked pussy and pressed his lips to her. He brushed the outer shell of her body, nibbling the puffy, sensitive flesh there with lazy slowness. It seemed he had all night to claim her, so he was in no rush.

He had braced her inner thighs with his hands and now his fingers massaged the tense flesh there gently, working in time with his wicked mouth.

"You accused me of teasing when I removed my clothing,"

Cassandra panted, trying to lift her hips and force his movement, even though she couldn't. "Now you do the same and
more to me!"

He glanced up at her again, more wicked than ever. "Are
you saying, my dear, that you would like me to do this?"

He slipped his hands higher and peeled her flushed skin
open wide, revealing the pearly flesh of her pussy.

"And this?" he continued, before he bent his head and found
her clit with his tongue. He swirled it around and around the
hard nub of flesh, coaxing it to full attention, torturing her
with the shocks of focused pleasure that such quick and focused sucking caused.

"Then this?" he murmured between licks. He pushed two
thick fingers into her sheath, spreading and nudging her tight
channel open, rubbing against the hidden bundle of nerves
that were just inside the opening.

"Yes!" she cried out, her head thrashing on the pillows as
intense pressure built low in her belly. She was going to come
and it was going to feel so good.

But then, just as swiftly as he had driven into her with his
mouth and touch, he stopped and pulled away.

"Too bad, sweetling," he purred as he went back to the
frustrating nuzzling. "I'm not ready to let you have your pleasure yet. And there's not a damn thing you can do about it.
You're not in control anymore."

Cassandra cried out again, but this time in frustration, as
Nathan traced the crease of her sex with just the tip of his
tongue and stroked her inner thighs gently.

"How long could I keep you this way?" he murmured, his fingers opening her a second time. "All night? All day tomorrow? Could I keep you on the edge forever, begging me?"

Cassandra squeezed her eyes shut, not wanting to admit anything to this man with his twisted agenda. She couldn't even tell him the truth, which was that only he could bring her to the brink so swiftly. And only he could keep her there, anxious and needy—forever, if he chose to do so. Her body still responded to him in a way it never had to other men, even the ones who had given her great pleasure.

With Nathan it was obsession. A need so powerful and pure that it took her breath away. It frightened her.

"You . . . you never talked during sex before," she panted, trying to maintain focus when Nathan began to stroke one finger along the slick flesh between her thighs.

He lifted his gaze briefly. "I guess you weren't the only one who learned new talents while we were apart, sweet."

Cassandra swallowed. The idea of him with other women both aroused and troubled her. Had he loved any of them? Or just used them to forget her? What had they looked like? Did she live up to their memories?

Had they lived up to hers?

He suddenly forced a long finger inside her body and her mind emptied of those questions.

"Pulse around me, angel," he growled, as he curled his finger seductively. "Ask me for what you want with that tight little body of yours."

Since she couldn't move any other part of her, Cassandra

had no choice but to surrender to his order. She tightened her sheath around his finger, squeezing her internal muscles in an even rhythm, silently begging for more than he was willing to share.

He let out a low curse and then his mouth dropped down. Once again he found her swollen clitoris and sucked it gently, swirling his tongue around and around the little nub until Cassandra dug her nails into her palms and cried out with the pure, unadulterated pleasure of his fingers and mouth.

Her cries grew louder, her arms and legs strained tighter against the bonds, and her body began to flutter in the uncontrolled prelude to release.

"Come for me," Nathan murmured against her flesh.

She could do nothing else but obey. Her skin grew hot and tight as wave after wave of unbelievable, harsh, hard pleasure rocked through her. But bending to his will did nothing to make him merciful. Instead of easing up in his sensual torture, Nathan quickened his licks, increased the pressure of his questing finger, ratcheting Cassandra's intense orgasm up and up until she thought her entire body might burst into flame and disappear.

The pleasure stretched out, seemed to go on forever, until she could hardly bear it. And then, slowly, the clenching tremors subsided, her breath slowed, and the cries from her raw throat quieted to low moans as the last vestiges of her orgasm faded away.

Nathan withdrew his wet finger and sat up, leaving her cold after such a heated encounter. He stared down at her, lips wet and flushed from his effort and eyes still glittering with just as much sensual promise as they had when he began.

Cassandra let her breath out in a shuttering sigh of both relief and frustration. They weren't anywhere close to being finished. It was patently clear that Nathan had so much more in store for her this night.

The torment had only just begun.

Chapter Six

If Cassandra lifted her head from the pillows, she could see Nathan's erection, still bold and strong against his belly. If anything, he looked even harder than before. More ready than ever to continue with his overpowering seduction. She shivered in anticipation.

He leaned forward, partially covering her with his broad chest. Cassandra couldn't hold back a little moan of excitement. He was going to fill her now, face to face, kissing her until she could taste her own arousal. Filling her until she begged for release, again and again.

But instead, he snapped the restraints around her wrists free. She lowered her aching arms and stared up at him in question as he leaned over her, his face inches from hers. She lifted her hands to cup his face, but he caught her wrists and held her down.

"You aren't in control, Cassandra," he whispered. "I am."

Before she could respond, he moved away, down her body to free her ankles. She watched him, tense and questioning, as he tossed the restraints away. He remained kneeling on the bed for a moment, watching her.

"Roll over," he said, refusing to meet her eyes.

She stifled a sigh. Being taken from behind was highly pleasurable, of course. It was a position that almost always led to her orgasm. But since their reunion, Nathan had refused to hold her while he made love to her.

He didn't want to look at her face. He wanted to punish her. Still.

Without comment, she did as he required, bracing her weight on her forearms as she lifted herself up for his perusal, touch, and taking. But instead of his fingers against her pussy, as she had expected, she sucked in a breath when Nathan began to gently stroke along the tight little hole of her backside.

She looked over her shoulder.

"Nathan?" she murmured, but he didn't respond. Instead, he began to rub the hot juices from her sex to lubricate the tiny opening.

"So tense," he murmured. "Don't tell me that the master lover is afraid of this."

She bit her lip, but remained silent. She had experienced

many acts in her years as a mistress. Things that would make her blush if she were forced to recite them. But this was the one thing she had denied her former lovers. The only thing she had never tried. And while she couldn't deny that it felt so good for Nathan to touch her in that untried, virgin place, she *was* afraid.

When she didn't answer, Nathan stopped stroking her and looked up to meet her eyes as she stared at him over her shoulder. "Cassandra?"

She shook her head slowly. "I . . . I haven't ever . . ."

His eyes widened and then a slow smile curled his lips. "Really." He seemed to say it more for his own benefit than for hers, for the word wasn't a question but a statement.

"How interesting. So I was your first in one way and I would be your first in this way, as well."

Cassandra squeezed her eyes shut, but she nodded.

Nathan was quiet and still for a moment, but then he curled his body up around hers and leaned down to press a hot, wet kiss against that sensitive spot on her spine that always drove her wild. She didn't think any of her other lovers had ever quite found it, but when Nathan did, her body jolted.

"I'm going to make this so good for you," he murmured. "And you know you cannot deny me any demand."

Cassandra let her breath out in a long sigh. He was right about that. And in truth, her heart was pounding as much from pure exhilaration at the thought of what he wanted to do as it was from anxiety.

"Then do it," she said, her voice a taunt. "If you say you

may take anything, why bother to pretend you are asking me my leave."

He caught her chin and tilted her face so that she looked at him over her shoulder, their gazes locked in combat.

"I'll have you begging, Cassandra," he growled. "Not asking."

She pulled her face away and arched against him as answer, grinding her still wet sheath against the granite length of his cock. He sucked in his breath at the touch, pressing forward almost as if against his will and letting his cock enter her just an inch. Her breath quickened with excitement at the breach, as did his.

Then he pulled back, shaking his head, and returned to the work of lubricating her untried bottom with the hot juices of her own body. The more he worked his fingers around the tight entrance, the more Cassandra began to relax and even enjoy the light touch. The area had so many nerves, so many points of pleasure she had never explored, that she couldn't help but gasp and cry out in wonder every time he stroked some hidden place of pleasure.

And then, suddenly and without warning, his finger glided inside her virgin channel. She caught her breath at the unexpected invasion, tensing as pleasure met a hint of pain. With his free hand, Nathan massaged her lower back, the brush of his skin gentle against hers as he murmured low words of comfort.

She shut her eyes, breathing as she tried to relax, tried to focus on the pleasure of the way he was gently stretching her, readying her for him, seducing her the very same way he had the first time they made love all those years ago. Then she had been a shy virgin, thrilled with the attention of such a handsome, charming man.

Now she felt the same way, despite years of experience, despite the painful past that she kept locked inside her, never to be revealed, especially to Nathan. But right now, with him coaxing her to a new pleasure, she felt pure again, new to pleasure. New to him.

"God, you are so tight, so hot," he moaned. "You are going to feel so fucking good."

She rocked herself back, a silent demand for more and he slipped his fingers from her body as he positioned the head of his cock at her entrance. She slowed her breath, forcing control over her anxiety as he began to slide inside. She had been well lubricated by his ministrations and she was surprised by how slick he slid into her, stretching her untried passage with his thick length.

She bit out a breath on a cry, overcome by the border between pleasure and pain, rocking on the edge and loving every unexpected moment.

When he was fully seated deep within her, he paused, letting her become acclimated to the new sensations. She bit her lip and rocked forward, reveling in the slide of skin on skin, then pushed back. He took her cue immediately and began to slowly thrust.

Cassandra was amazed by how quickly her tense, frightened body relaxed into the new feelings. Pain was forgotten as Nathan took her in this new way, pleasure was all that remained as his thrusts grew harder, faster.

Her tingling pussy clenched at emptiness each time he thrust, jealously aching as she was taken. Bracing one arm on the headrest above her, Cassandra snaked her fingers down to her wet body and began to rub her clit in time to his thrusts. He seemed to quicken in response, and she rushed to keep up with him.

Then, as suddenly as he began, Nathan stopped moving. She let out a strangled moan of desperation as she shifted back to take what he now withheld. He moaned before he wrapped one arm around her hips and held her steady.

"Wait," he whispered, his voice thick with the strain of doing just that.

"Why?" she moaned, the sound closer to a wail than a whisper.

He shifted and his cock moved inside of her, eliciting a harsh groan from her throat as she watched him reach out and grasp the glass dildo that now rested at a precarious angle on her bedside table. It was one of the few toys that hadn't fallen to the floor when he swept her bed clean.

He pushed the toy into her hand. "Use it," he growled close to her ear.

Cassandra gasped as she took the item. She craned her neck to look back at him. His eyes were dilated with pleasure and lit with pure challenge.

"Now," he ordered, as he gripped her hips and plunged even deeper into her clenching body.

She jolted, her hands shaking as she lowered the toy between her legs. The next time he withdrew, she glided the smooth glass surface into her pussy. It slid home easily, as she was still soaked from his eager tongue.

Nathan drove forward again and they let out a cry in tandem. Cassandra's head lolled back. This was bliss, pure pleasure. To be filled so completely, to be taken in such a way . . .

It was heaven.

"Don't stop," she cried out as she arched her hips wildly and starting to thrust the glass toy in and out of her sheath.

Nathan cursed and then he did what she asked. Their bodies moved in time, their sweat mingling, cries and moans echoing as they moved in tandem toward a pleasure so powerful that Cassandra feared she might not survive it once it arrived.

Until it did.

The dam within her broke as Nathan flexed his hips in a slow circle. Her pussy began to shiver, wet heat pouring down the toy inside of her to coat her fingers as the pleasure that had been coiling ever tighter and tighter finally sprung free.

Cassandra slammed her free hand against the bed as she cried out Nathan's name over and over, she thrust back against him in a wild rhythm, driven to the brink of madness by pleasure. The orgasm seemed to go on forever, long past the point where she was so weak that she could hardly keep her body in position.

And Nathan was no more immune to the outrageous explosion than she was. The moment her body pulsed, he let out a roar and she felt his essence pump inside of her as he thrust wildly against her.

They finally collapsed against the sweaty coverlet, his

body curled around hers, her arms shaking from release. She moaned as she gently removed the glass dildo from inside her still-tremoring sheath and set it aside. Nathan didn't move to release her, so she curled her arms around his and held him against her for the first time in what seemed like forever.

"Well," he finally said, as he coaxed her onto her back so that he could peer down into her face. His expression was hooded and unreadable, even though he was so close. "There is one more thing no other man can say they had from you first."

Cassandra pursed her lips, not only from displeasure at his crass comment, but also to stop herself from responding. The last thing she should do was to remind this man that he was the first one for *everything* important in her life.

He had been her first lover. Her first love. Honestly, he was the *only* man she had ever loved. Her feelings for her other lovers had never been more than fleeting affection and desire.

Nathan was her first heartbreak.

"Do you intend to engrave that somewhere, then?" she asked, pushing off the bed. Lying in his arms was a false comfort. She had to be careful that she didn't start to believe it. "Tell the world that you are the first everything for the famous Cassandra Willows?"

Before he replied, he watched as she donned the satin robe that hung beside her door and tied it at her waist. He made no effort to cover himself the same way, and she found herself stealing a side-glance at his impressive body.

Damn him for keeping time as his mistress and not becoming her slave. It would be so much easier to hate him if he had gotten uglier.

He shrugged one shoulder. "The fact that *you* know I had first claim on every part of your body is good enough for me. Whatever else you do, whoever else you turn to after this is over, you cannot erase that."

"You are correct," she said softly, turning to the mirror at her dressing table rather than face him. In the reflection, she saw the haggard lines of her own face, the sadness she hoped he would never see. "No matter how much I try to forget, that much is true."

He sat up. "Do you try to forget often? Does that make the fact that you lied, that you threw away love, easier?"

She spun around to find that he had already begun dressing. His mouth was a thin line of displeasure and his eyes were narrow and hard as he thrust one leg, then the other into his trousers.

Her hands were shaking as she stared at him.

"You don't have any idea of my heart, Nathan. Or what makes my life easier or more difficult. You think you do, but you have no idea why . . ."

She broke off before she said too much. Years ago, she had vowed that it would not be she who offered an explanation to Nathan Manning if he ever did step foot back into her life. She had done nothing wrong, she had *nothing* to explain.

Besides, his knowing the truth of what had happened to her that night so long ago wouldn't change the past. And she had a sneaking suspicion it might destroy him. No matter what lay between them, she didn't relish the idea that she could be the one who did that.

"Why what?" he asked, coming toward her without buttoning his shirt. "Pray, do explain yourself, if you can, Cassandra."

She shook her head. "You know everything already, don't you? Why bother hearing me when you already have the truth in your palm?"

He shook his head, his expression heavy with disgust as he finished dressing. The silence stretched between them, with Cassandra fighting not to watch him, he keeping his gaze on his task until he was finally back to being the cold lord of the manor who had come demanding she bow to his will.

The heated, passionate lover was gone.

"I will be back," he finally barked, as he made his way to the door. When he reached it, he gave her a look so wintry that the room seemed to drop in temperature. "Be ready."

Before she could answer, he was gone, the door slamming behind him hard enough that the picture on the wall beside it shivered.

Frustration mounting, Cassandra caught the nearest thing at hand, her hairbrush, and hurtled it across the room. It bounced off the door with a loud bump and then skidded away in the opposite direction.

She sighed. There was no satisfaction in throwing things, or screaming, or doing anything else.

Until Nathan returned, there would be no satisfaction at all.

Chapter Seven

Music filled the room, dancers spun around him, women flirted with him with open intent . . . and yet Nathan could hardly attend to the ball. His mind was addled with thoughts of Cassandra, just as it had been for the two long days he had avoided her.

He told himself that he was pulling away from her because he wanted her to squirm, to wonder when and if he would return and what his demands would be when he did.

That was part of it, of course. But in reality, their last encounter had been so emotionally intense that he felt the thin wire of his control strain almost to the point of breaking. With Cassandra, that was a very dangerous thing. He needed a break to regroup.

And so he was here at a ball hosted by the Earl and Countess of Rothschild. Hating every moment of it. He had never been much for these events, even before he met Cassandra. He found most debutantes to be empty shells, and their mamas too clinging and demanding. The wine was never strong enough, the music too loud, and the crowds overpowering.

Tonight, though, those things were especially unbearable because this ball was hosted by a man who had intimate knowledge of Cassandra—as intimate as his own.

Nathan's thoughts were interrupted by a female voice from behind him. "Lord Blackhearth, how good of you to come."

Nathan turned and found himself face to face with his host and hostess. Lady Rothschild was as beautiful as all the *ton* raged that she was, with fair blond hair and the brightest, clearest blue eyes he had ever seen. She was draped in fine silk—a gown Nathan suddenly wondered if Cassandra had designed, with sparkling diamonds at her wrist, her ears, and around her neck.

It was well known that Rothschild doted on the woman, completely smitten with her since they wed. It certainly seemed to be so true, as Rothschild gave his wife a look of pure adoration before he focused his attention on Nathan.

"Yes, so good of you to join our party, Blackhearth," he said with a friendly nod.

Nathan bit his lip hard and forced himself to hold out a hand to this man, this handsome man who had once had a flagrant reputation for womanizing and sin.

This man who had once had a short, torrid affair with Cassandra, and still frequented her shop, both for her gowns for his wife and for her toys . . . God only knew who those were for.

Nathan wanted nothing more than to punch the other man square in the jaw . . . and yet he couldn't. Rothschild was too powerful to make an enemy. Even if he wasn't, Nathan didn't want his sad obsession with Cassandra to become public knowledge.

"Thank you for inviting me," he forced himself to say through clenched teeth. "Being back in London for such a short time, I fear I am woefully out of touch with Society. It is a great pleasure to have the chance to meet with old friends again."

Rothschild smiled as he motioned for a servant with a tray of red wine. As he offered a glass to Nathan, he lifted his own in Nathan's direction.

"And make new ones, I hope. I hear you and I have some similar interests."

Nathan all but choked on his wine at the unexpected comment. Was Rothschild being so crass as to bring up Cassandra right here, in front of his supposedly beloved wife?

Nathan shot a glance to Lady Rothschild. The woman smiled at him, but it wasn't the empty expression of a vapid lady who had no idea of her husband's activities outside of their "happy" home.

"To what are you referring, my lord?" he asked, wary.

"You made some investments during your time in India, did you not?" Rothschild tilted his head. "Silks, spices, and the like? I, too, have some holdings there, but I'd like to increase my investments. I would greatly enjoy speaking to you about the country, getting your opinion on new ventures there, as well as hearing about your experiences. My wife and I are always searching for new adventures."

Miranda Hamon smiled up at her husband again, but this time Nathan sensed something unexpected in her expression. Passion. Desire. Deep and abiding love.

Nathan snapped his gaze away. When they looked at each other like that, it made him feel like an intruding outsider to their happiness.

"Of course, Rothschild, I would be happy to discuss my travels with you."

That was a lie. Nathan didn't really want to talk about India with this man, but he nodded his head regardless. At least the other man *wasn't* blatantly pointing out their shared lover, as he had originally believed.

But then, when he considered the topic rationally, there was no reason for the earl to know that Nathan also shared an interest in Cassandra. The two of them hadn't made their relationship so public before she threw him aside. Thank God for that.

Nathan looked around the room absently, hoping to find a way to politely escape this conversation. It was very difficult to look the other man in the eye when he knew Rothschild had been intimate with Cassandra. All he could think about was the distasteful picture of the two of them tangled in an embrace, of Cassandra moaning and coming the same way she had done for him a few days before.

"How long did you live in India, my lord?" Lady Rothschild

asked. "You are the talk of London, but no one speaks of the interesting facts like why you left Society and how long you explored the world."

Nathan shot another glance her way. There was a laughing sparkle in her eyes that was almost impossible not to return, and an intelligence that actually put him to mind of Cassandra, though the women couldn't have been more different in appearance. Miranda Hamon was all slender, willowy loveliness, while Cassandra was curvy and delicious. Yet both were sharp, attractive women who exuded confidence. Seeing Miranda Hamon made Nathan wonder just what kind of woman Cassandra would have become had she not refused him. What kind of Countess?

He shook the thought away with determination.

"The talk of London?" he forced a smile. "Surely you exaggerate."

The woman laughed, and she seemed to glow from within. "Most certainly I do not, and I think you know it full well. You are a novelty, a prodigal son returned to the fold and *they* cannot get enough of you."

Nathan shrugged one shoulder. She was right, of course, and that played perfectly into his plans. He would find a wife before the Season was out. By that time, he was certain his anger and desire for Cassandra would be purged and he could get on with things—like creating heirs and spares, and preparing for the inevitable time when his father would be gone and he'd become a powerful Marquis.

"I would be remiss if I did not offer to introduce you to a

few of our eligible female guests and their chaperones," Lady Rothschild continued, with a wave of her hand around the room. "Is there any woman in particular who strikes your fancy?"

Nathan glanced around him. He had been carefully considering the women in attendance since his arrival. Certainly, there were plenty of beautiful women to pick amongst in every corner of the crowded room, from the experienced widows who sent him blatant looks of invitation to the sweetest innocents who still believed in fairytale princes. If he wished it, tonight he could find a lover, a mistress, or even a wife if he turned in the correct direction.

And yet there wasn't one woman in the room who caught his eye or kept his attention as much as the redheaded seamstress he was blackmailing.

What a sickness this desire was.

"I am afraid I do not know any of the young ladies well enough yet to choose one over another," he stammered finally, as Miranda Hamon tilted her head in unspoken question when he was silent too long. "Which lady would *you* chose for me?"

"Oh, the power, sir!" Rothschild laughed, as he sipped his drink. "You do not know what you are saying when you give my wife carte blanche with your future."

Lady Rothschild laughed at his teasing as she released her husband's arm. "Ethan is correct, though he is dastardly to point it out. You put far too much faith in my ability to match you when we have just met and I know nothing of your pursuits, or personality, or interests. But I *could* introduce you to Miss Rebecca Ward. She is a favorite of all the gentlemen this Season. She and her mother are standing there with Mr. Stephan Undercliffe."

Nathan stiffened at the mention of the other man's name. Great God, Undercliffe was another of Cassandra's former lovers. Was the party filled with men who had spent nights tangled with her sweet body? Did they all belong to some kind of sick club in which he was now eligible for membership?

The very idea turned his stomach, even as he followed with his gaze the direction Miranda had indicated with one slender hand. Two women stood with a dark-haired man, but he hardly noticed them. He was too focused on Undercliffe.

So, this was Cassandra's former lover. Well, she never chose an unattractive one, that was certain. Undercliffe was very tall, with a wicked smile that spoke volumes about his character even before Nathan had spoken a word to him.

"What do you think?"

Nathan shook his head. Lady Rothschild wasn't asking his opinion of Undercliffe, but of the young lady with whom the bastard was conversing. Finally, he forced his attention to the girl. She was a very pretty young lady at that, and yet still Nathan felt no interest stir in his belly at all.

"Perhaps it is too soon to think about pursuit," he said, trying to be polite. There was no reason to be rude to Lady Rothschild, even if he could scarce stand the sight of her husband and wanted to run screaming from her ballroom like a madman. "I have just returned, after all."

The Countess stared at him for a long moment, but then she smiled slightly. "Very well. If you change your mind, do let me know."

"My dear, I think the gentleman may already have a lady in his sights," Rothschild interrupted with a chuckle. "Do you not recognize the wild expression in his eyes?"

Nathan stiffened. Well, that was just about enough coming from this man. He had no intention of discussing his current female pursuits with Rothschild.

"Thank you again for your kindness, my lord, my lady. I am afraid that I must cry off early. Good evening."

Then he turned on his heel and stalked away.

After he was out of earshot, Miranda turned to Ethan with a small smile. "What in the world did you do to him, my love?"

Her husband's eyes widened. "What do you mean?"

"He could hardly look at you. Perhaps you did something wretched to him before I reformed you." She looked at him, all innocence, though she knew what such a comment would incite.

Ethan caught her around the waist and drew her closer, close enough that she felt the insistent pressure of his desire against her belly. "Who says I'm reformed?"

She shut her eyes with a tiny groan. "I don't think anyone is in the orangery."

And they slipped from the crowd and never thought of Nathan Manning again.

★ ★ ★

The night outside was inky dark, the clouds too heavy to let the moon pierce through. Cassandra rested her chin in her palm as she stared with unseeing eyes out her window. She hardly noticed when the parlor door opened beside her until her best friend spoke and startled her from her troubling, distracting reverie.

"I'm glad to see you are taking a break," Elinor said, as she entered the room bearing a tray with tea and a towering mound of Cassandra's favorite biscuits. "You have been so odd the last few days."

Cassandra forced a tight smile and stared at the cookies that now tempted her from the small table beside her chair. Apparently, she was not hiding her troubled mood as well as she had hoped. Not only had Elinor noticed her distraction, but the cook was clearly concerned for her, too. She only baked the chocolate wonders when Cassandra was sick or sad.

If her friends and servants could see her heart so clearly, that probably meant that Nathan recognized how much their "reunion" troubled her, too. And that meant he had the upper hand in every way.

Perfect.

She snatched a pastry from the tray and ate half of it in one big bite. Elinor tilted her head and looked at her with an expression laced with real concern before she took a place on the settee beside her.

"Do you want to talk to me about whatever is troubling you? We have always been honest with each other and helped one another when we could. You seem like you need that now more than ever." Elinor covered Cassandra's hand gently. "Is it your work? Are you too overwhelmed? I can try to manage your schedule differently and give you more time away. Perhaps you could go to Bath and enjoy the waters for a few days."

Cassandra let her eyes flutter shut. The idea of running away, hiding out, and pampering herself was tempting. She couldn't help but picture herself lounging in the warm springs of Bath . . . except an unbidden image of Nathan intruded, even in her fantasy. Entering the water, opening her legs, filling her with more heat and steam than the hottest tub . . .

With a shiver, she shook her head and tried to forget the erotic image. "No, if I have troubles, they have nothing to do with my work."

In fact, her occupation was the only thing keeping her sane at present. When she sewed or designed gowns, she was able to quiet the memories of Nathan's touch, if only temporarily. The worries she felt about how long his quest for vengeance would last, the fear that if she let herself, she could easily remember what it was like to care for the man, despite all her reasons to maintain distance, faded just a little.

Designing her toys had become a bit more complicated. Every time she molded an item made for sin, she couldn't help but picture using it with Nathan. Memories of their hot encounter a few days ago invariably came flooding back to distract and distress her.

"Then it must be a man," her friend said with a sigh, intruding upon Cassandra's sensual reverie. "Although I have never seen you so forlorn over a lover before, or be so secretive as to keep a new tryst quiet, even from me. You do not have to tell me his name, but if you would like to talk about him . . ."

Cassandra shoved the other half of the cookie into her mouth and chewed thoughtfully. Elinor was correct that she had never hidden her lovers in the past. She wasn't ashamed of what she had done and with whom. Sometimes it was quite . . . *invigorating* to whisper her naughtiest secrets to her best friend, reliving the memories with each word. It invariably led to a satisfying round of self-pleasure later in her chamber, and she had the sneaking suspicion that the same was true for the more sheltered Elinor.

But with Nathan, everything was different. In all the years since they met, she had never spoken to anyone about their past relationship. She had never given away the facts of their sexual encounters. It seemed too personal, too emotional to gossip about the details of the way he touched her, the way he moved his mouth over her skin.

She swallowed the delicious biscuit and shrugged one shoulder. "There isn't a man."

Her friend arched a brow. "Yes, there is. Your servants have been buzzing about someone who comes here and is able to make any demand he wants and you don't argue. And you have the look of a woman mooning over a man who has left her well-pleasured." Her friend stared at her harder. "The fact that you deny he exists tells me a great deal. Is he of such importance that you try to protect his reputation?"

Cassandra picked at her skirt, dropping her gaze so that

her friend wouldn't see. "I really don't want to discuss him."

Elinor pursed her lips in a thin line. "But this secret is hurting you; that much is plain. This man must have an enormous amount of power if he—"

Her friend broke off with a gasp, as she covered her lips with one hand and stared.

"What is it?" Cassandra asked, dreading the answer.

Elinor lowered her fingers to whisper, "Good God, Cass, you aren't sleeping with the Prince Regent, are you?"

Her friend's tone was one of utter disgust, and Cassandra couldn't blame her. The idea of anyone finding the fat, pompous leader attractive was a bit much for her.

"Of course not!" she snapped, glaring at her friend. "Give me some credit for taste!"

"Then someone else," her friend pressed. "Someone in parliament or a man with a reputation for piety?"

Cassandra shook her head and sighed. Now her friend was so concerned that it was going to be virtually impossible to put her off the topic.

"It isn't like that at all. The problem isn't that his standing must be upheld or anything of that sort. I . . . I . . ." she hesitated. Elinor was the closest thing to family she had and she ached to tell someone about her woes—all of them. They hurt so much to keep inside.

"I knew him before I came here," she found herself whispering. "It was so long ago and we were both very different then. We shared something special . . . or I *thought* it was special. Now he is back in my life and everything is complicated by the past."

"So you are in love," her friend said, as she slowly got to her feet and backed away a long step. She blinked down at Cassandra in disbelief. "You are finally in love."

"No." Cassandra pushed to her own feet and strode as far across the room as she could. "That is the most foolish thing I've ever heard. Of course I'm not in love with him. Once, perhaps, I thought I was, but—"

"Ha!" Her friend pursued her around the room like a bull-dog. "So you *did* care for him deeply."

"Yes—" Cassandra began, but Elinor was still talking.

"No woman ever fully overcomes such a thing; trust that I know that from personal experience. You may deny your feelings, but the fact that you have allowed this man back into your life, that you have allowed him to barge into your home whenever he likes, that you—"

Cassandra squeezed her eyes shut. "Elinor, he is blackmailing me."

The interruption cut her friend off short and stopped her dead in her tracks.

"I . . . I don't understand," she finally said, after a long, silent moment.

Cassandra sighed. It was bad enough that Stephan knew part of the truth; now she was going to have to reveal her humiliation to her best friend, as well.

"He hates me for something that occurred in our past," she explained, hoping her own emotions on that score weren't obvious. "And yet he still wants me. So he is blackmailing me into an affair. If I do not do as he requires, he will destroy my reputation."

"How?"

She squeezed her eyes shut for a brief moment, fully aware of how unpleasant this conversation was about to become. "He'll reveal my secondary business to the matrons of the *ton* in such a way that will make it impossible for them to ignore it."

"Oh, great God," her friend whispered. "How does he know? We have always been so careful!"

Cassandra expelled a humorless laugh. "Not careful enough, I suppose. He has been planning this for so long, I expect he has had spies watching me almost from the moment we parted."

And yet he still didn't have an inkling of the truth about why she hadn't eloped with him that long ago night.

"We must stop him," her friend said, rushing forward and catching Cassandra's hands before she could move away. "You have friends of influence; surely they would help you if they were told you were being forced into sex by some fiend."

Cassandra did wrench her hands away now and staggered backward. Elinor had no idea of the memories those words inspired, and she struggled to keep them at bay.

"He may be blackmailing me," she panted, her voice strained and odd to her own ears. "But he isn't forcing me into sex."

She might accuse Nathan of many things, but rape was not one of them.

"Oh." Her friend stared at her like she didn't understand, and Cassandra felt for her. She wasn't sure she understood her own motivations, either. She wanted Nathan, but she hated his blackmail. She ached for his touch, but she feared the feelings it inspired. She wanted him to come back to her, and she feared he would.

Her life, in short, was upside down and sideways, completely out of control.

"What can I do?" Elinor asked, her voice quiet and calm, the same tone she used when Cassandra was panicking over deadlines or behind on an important project.

Cassandra smiled, despite her own pain and confusion, before she wrapped her arms around her friend and squeezed. She did adore Elinor like she was her own sister. "Nothing, I'm afraid. He hasn't been back here in two days. Perhaps he is finished with me. He's bored of me already and feels his revenge is complete."

While that should have been a comforting thought, it was anything but, because Cassandra still ached for him. Despite everything, when she thought of him never coming back it made her tremble with disappointment and longing.

Her friend's eyes lit up with hope, but before Elinor could respond, the door to the parlor opened. Almost as though their discussion of him had called him to her, Nathan stood in the entryway. She sucked in a breath of surprise and relief. So it wasn't over yet. Not by a long shot, judging by the way his eyes glowed with need and his body was taut with tension.

And despite herself, Cassandra was flooded with answering desire. She wanted to wrap herself around him, draw him deep inside of her. She wanted to fill herself with him in every way.

Until Elinor shrugged from her arms and said, "*You* must be the bastard who is blackmailing my best friend. Tell me, sir, does it make you feel like more of a man to take what you want like a brute?"

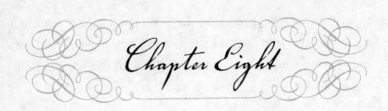

Chapter Eight

Although Cassandra had been hugging a young woman when he burst into her parlor, Nathan had hardly noticed the other person who was now a part of the moment between them. All he saw, when he opened the door, was *her*.

He soaked in every inch of her, from her less-than-fashionable flannel gown to her red hair bound loosely at the nape of her neck. She looked so much like the girl he had once wanted to possess in every way and she was the only important person in the room . . . in the *world* at that moment.

Until her friend turned on him, a light of pure hatred in her eyes, and said words laced with poison.

"*You* must be the bastard who is blackmailing my best friend. Tell me, sir, does it make you feel like more of a man to take what you want like a brute?"

He folded his arms and looked past his attacker at Cassandra. She was frozen, her face bloodless, as she stared back at him. Was *that* what Cassandra had told this shaking, angry woman who was now crossing the room toward him in a way that could only be described as threatening, even though the dark-haired beauty was so slender that he could probably break her over his knee?

Still, the other woman approached like a leopard in India protecting her threatened cub. "Are you going to answer me, sir?" she asked.

He cocked a brow. It wasn't often that he threw the weight of his position around, but this seemed the perfect time. "Do you know who I am?"

"If you are indeed the person threatening my friend," the woman snapped, her eyes narrowed, "I don't care about anything else."

He smiled at her, thin and just as threatening as her posture. "I am Nathan Manning, Earl of Blackhearth. Someday I will be Marquis Herstale. And you are?"

The young woman stopped when he listed off his present and future titles. Now it was Elinor's face that grew still and pale as she spun back on Cassandra, with a gasp. She nodded slightly, as if she was verifying everything he said. When her friend turned back, there was more wariness in her stare, but no less hatred and accusation.

"Whether you are lord or servant, you have no right to force Cassandra to your will," she said, this time much more softly.

Surprise made Nathan rock back. Few people would be so bold as to maintain their loyalty in the face of the subtle threat of his position. He couldn't help but respect this young woman for doing so, though he felt her choice of friends was dubious. Would Cassandra remain so true if the roles were reversed?

The young woman folded her arms. "If you would like to pursue some kind of revenge on me for my impertinence, then I gladly give you my name, for I don't fear bullies. I am Elinor Clifford. And Cassandra Willows is the best friend I have ever had in my life."

Nathan considered the woman for a long moment, then shrugged one shoulder. "I once said the same thing about Cassandra, but then she proved me a fool. Certainly, though, I admire your loyalty to a woman who has demonstrated she can lie with ease."

Elinor let out another sound of utter outrage, but before she could launch into a fresh defense of her friend, Nathan lifted a dismissive hand to silence her.

"This is not a battle for you to fight, dear lady. I would suggest you run along and let Cassandra protect herself." He locked gazes with Cassandra. "She is well capable of it."

Elinor Clifford's mouth thinned to an iron line, but she didn't respond. Instead, she shot her friend a look over her shoulder. This time, Cassandra moved forward slightly.

"Go, Elinor," she said quietly, but her stare never left his face. "You should know me well enough to know I can handle myself. There is no need for you to insert yourself in this conflict. As his lordship suggests, it is between us. Only we can resolve it." She arched a brow and a sultry light entered her eyes that made his stomach clench yet again with unwanted, uncontrolled desire. "One way or another."

Elinor hesitated, but then she nodded. "If you need me, please call, Cassandra."

Then she swept from the room and didn't give even a passing glance toward him as she slammed the door behind her, her final comment on his presence there.

Once she was gone, Nathan found himself watching Cassandra. He didn't even know why he was here. After he left the Rothschild ball, he had found himself driving around and around the city, lost and unsure of much except that he wanted to see her. Only when he had surrendered to his weakness and given his driver the direction to her home had he felt any kind of peace.

Yes, peace. Not his usual anger or drive for revenge, or anything else. The sense of calm was far more troubling than the other emotions.

"Did you tell your friend that I was forcing myself on you?" he asked, watching Cassandra carefully for her reaction.

She flinched and there was a powerful pain in her stare before she turned it away so he could no longer read her heart. So, she didn't like being caught in her lies and false implications.

"Of course not," she whispered, her voice harsh. "In fact, I told her myself that blackmail or not, you could not force me to do anything I did not myself desire. I don't think you would press or force me if I truly resisted you. You are not that kind of man, no matter what else you have become or try to be when you are here with me."

He moved toward her on that confession. For once, he actually believed her, as foolish as that might be, and he was pleased she hadn't claimed he was some kind of rapist.

"So you admit you want me," he said softly, reaching for her when he was close enough. He tangled a loose lock of her hair around his finger and brushed it away from her face. "That you would be with me even if there was no blackmail."

She lifted her gaze and, to his surprise, her eyes sparkled like she was holding back tears. "Don't make me say it."

He slipped his fingers deep into the silky warmth of her hair, cupping her head and tilting it up to give himself full access to her lips, her elegant throat.

"What if I told you that I long for you, despite everything? That I want you day and night, that you ruin all other women for me. Or that I want to kill with my bare hands any man who ever touched you. Tonight I had the opportunity not once, but twice, and it was quite tempting."

She sucked in a harsh breath and her lips parted with surprise at his candor. He would regret it later, he was sure, but for now the words continued to flow from his lips.

"Would knowing those things make it easier for you to admit that you want me deep inside of you?"

She swallowed hard and he watched her throat work with the action. Finally, she nodded, pulling her head against his hand with the jerky motion.

"Yes." Her voice barely carried, though they were not even an inch apart now. "I want you. I hoped to forget you, to stop this longing, but it never went away. Blackmail or not, when I saw you in your aunt's home, I hoped that I would return to your bed, at least one last time."

As he dropped his mouth to hers, Nathan recognized that she hadn't said she wanted to return to his life or his heart, just his bed. A small sting made itself clear, but he shoved it away. There was no future for them, he knew that full-well. He didn't want one. Just *this*.

This merging of mouths that was gentler than it had ever been before, a slow tangling of tongues and a soft clench of her fingers against his back as she wound her arms around him and clung tight to his neck.

He lifted her up, molding her body to his, as her slippered feet left the floor. It was like heaven to feel her breasts flattened against his chest, to hear her soft moans as they entered his mouth, to be engulfed by the heat of her body as she struggled to get even closer.

He carried her, still clinging to his shoulders, to the settee by the fire and laid her across the velvety cushions. She reached for him as he covered her, holding him against her body with a desperation that surprised him.

"Let me touch you this time," she whispered against his neck as she kissed him. "Let me see you. Don't deny me."

He was so lost in the haze of need that she was quickly creating in him that he almost lost the meaning of her plea. Almost. So his attempts to keep a distance between them *had* affected her in some way. He wasn't sure whether to be glad or sorry for that fact.

So he didn't choose. Tonight wasn't about the blackmail or the tangled, turbulent emotions she inspired deep within him. Tonight was just a moment stolen from time. Later he would return to control. He would latch back onto the past, the rage, the need to make and break this affair on his own terms.

Tonight he just wanted to touch this woman and allow her to touch him. He wanted to forget the agendas tonight, his own and hers, and simply remember the pleasure of holding her like he once did.

"Touch me," he growled, his voice rough.

She shoved at him, shifting him off her body, and making him sit up. Then she got to her knees on the settee beside him. There was a hungry, eager light that darkened her eyes to a lush, deep green—deeper than the jungle, darker than anything he'd ever seen.

She reached for him, unlooping his cravat with experienced fingers and spreading the fabric wide as she opened his buttons one by one. She slipped her fingers into the gap she had created and hissed out a sound of hot pleasure when she touched his skin.

He couldn't help but echo that sound. It had been so fucking long. He was just beginning to realize how long.

She shifted, skimming one leg over his so that she straddled his lap, her skirts piled awkwardly around her. But she didn't seem to care, she was too lost in gliding her hands up and down his chest, raking her nails over his sensitive skin, and popping the last remaining buttons of his tailored shirtwaist.

Cassandra shoved the fabric away, letting it smash behind them without finesse. She had lost all ability for self-control or elegance the moment she touched him. Unlike any other man who had ever shared her bed, Nathan swept her away. In all ways.

She arched up, cupping his cheeks to draw his mouth to hers. He tasted like scotch and heaven as their tongues collided in a gentle, exploring, and teasing war. She felt the hard length of him against her thigh and shivered.

Soon enough.

But in this moment where he allowed her every whim, she wasn't ready to surrender this tiny piece of power. Once this act of passion was over, she knew full well that he could—and probably would—return to the cold distance he had maintained with her so far. This might be her only chance to explore him, pleasure him, remember how good it felt to touch him.

She shimmied down, letting her knees rest on the floor between his legs. As she moved, she glided her mouth down his hot skin, licking the curve of his throat, sucking at the smooth skin along his collarbone, taking one flat male nipple into her mouth. He bucked when she suckled at him, his hips slamming into her as he released a needy moan.

She swelled with the power and pleasure of making him lose even that fraction of control. As much as he remembered her body, she recalled his. Like how sensitive he was when she kissed along his chest, glided down his stomach as she did now.

And she had a few more tricks now than she had as a shy girl. As she traced her tongue along his defined stomach, she began to work his trousers loose. With a few tugs, she slipped them down over his hips and his erection popped free.

She stopped kissing him and took a long, hot moment to stare. He was, by far, the most beautiful specimen of a man she had ever seen. His cock was perfectly formed, from the swollen mushroom head of it to the thick blade of the shaft. And when it was fully ready, just the sight of that big thrust of muscle made her pussy twinge and clench in anticipation of what he would do with it.

But she had never tasted him. That was one of the acts she had grown to love later, after he was gone. Now she wanted more than anything to take him deep into her throat, to make him moan and ache. To bring him hard, heavy pleasure.

She caught the hot length of him in her palm and they shivered together.

"You are so beautiful," she murmured, stroking him once, twice, smoothing away the tiny trickle of moisture that leaked from the tip of his cock.

He groaned as an answer, his head flopping back against the settee cushions. His neck strained and his breath was coming in pants. In short, he was utterly at her mercy.

And she loved it.

Dipping her head, she swirled the tip of her tongue around

him, tasting the salty bitterness, loving the velvet heat. He jolted at the contact and when she looked up, he was staring at her with wide eyes.

"Cass?" he rasped.

Now tears stung her eyes. That was the first time he had cut her name short, calling her by the nickname that only those closest to her used. The one he used to call out in pleasure and whisper in love.

"I want to pleasure you," she whispered back, returning her attention to his erection so that he wouldn't see her emotional response to his use of her name.

He didn't argue, only slowly lifted his hips so that his cock worked through her hand. She took that as an invitation and returned to her work. This time she didn't tease though. She sucked him deep within her mouth, loving how he filled her so completely. When he touched the back of her throat, she withdrew, sucking hard as she drew him out of her wet mouth. Thrusting like he would eventually do inside of her pussy, she worked at him.

He seemed to grow even bigger between her lips, hardening as he moaned and murmured nonsensical ramblings of desire.

It didn't take long for her to learn new things about his pleasure. How fast she could go before he trembled, how he liked the extra pressure of her tongue against the base of his cock when she fully seated him in her mouth. She made him tremble, she took him to the edge, she tormented him in the sweetest way possible.

But before she could feel the hot splash of his release, he jerked away from her mouth, his breath in hot pants. She looked up to find his expression wild and heated as he stared down at her.

"Not like that, Cass," he said, as he caught her beneath the arms and lifted her from her knees. "Inside of you."

She nodded in mute agreement, rising just long enough to strip out of her gown, her undergarments, and her stockings. He stared at her, his eyes glazed as she straddled him a second time, this time unimpeded by their clothing. His cock strained up, rubbing against her wet slit as she positioned herself above him.

He thrust up as she coaxed herself down, and their bodies merged with a heated slide of slick skin. Their shared moan echoed in the quiet room and Cassandra couldn't help but tilt her head back in pure pleasure. God, he felt so good inside of her, a stark reminder of how much she wanted him. Needed him.

Hadn't ever gotten enough of him.

She rocked forward out of instinct and desire, gliding his cock in and out of her with hard, clumsy thrusts of her hips. He seemed to share in her desperation, for he cupped her breasts, lifting their heavy weight together before he began to glide his lips back and forth from one taut nipple to the next. His chin was beginning to show the first signs of stubble and she cried out as the roughness caressed her.

"Still so sensitive," he murmured, as he lifted his hips in time to her thrusts.

Yes, he remembered everything, just as she did. The thought made her hips rock faster, racing toward the brink, reaching for the blind explosion of pleasure that was inevitable now that their bodies were joined so intimately. Her sheath began to tremble, the tingling awareness increasing with every long, hard thrust.

A rush of heat, a spasming of her inner muscles that was so intense it bordered on pain. She clung to his shoulders as wave after wave of pleasure rocked her, overwhelmed her. Her nails dug into his skin, but she couldn't stop it, her cries filled the air around them, but she couldn't be silent.

All she could do was quake, milking his cock with her pussy as her hot wetness flowed over him. She was aware of him through the explosion. She watched him through heavy lids as he fought to stay calm. Fought to keep himself from losing control. But the more her hips rocked, the harder her sheath worked him, the more obvious it became that he was going to lose the battle.

When he did, it was magnificent. He roared out her name, lifted his hips until she came off the settee and then he pulled himself away to pump his essence away from her body. The power of that moment drove Cassandra back into the heights of release and she cried out a second wail of pleasure that melded with his hoarse, animal cries in the parlor.

When the moment had finally passed, when the room began to refocus, Cassandra wrapped her arms around him and held tight. He didn't resist her embrace. In fact, they collapsed onto their sides on the settee, face to face, as the intense pleasure of their passionate joining faded into a background hum of relaxation and contentment.

Cassandra held back a sigh as Nathan's arms came around her, holding her against him and keeping her from tumbling off her precarious perch on the narrow settee. Although she couldn't have hurt herself with the short fall to the ground, it still felt like a protective gesture, something gentle and caring.

She wasn't a fool. This unexpected respite from Nathan's vicious attempts at revenge was in no way permanent. They had resolved nothing, even if this joining was far more intense and emotional than any time they had sex before.

And yet she remained snuggled against his chest, breathing in the musky scent of his skin. Until he turned away, she intendend to enjoy this moment. Later she could convince herself it meant nothing.

Nathan brushed her tangled hair away from her face with the back of his hand, the touch warm on her skin. She glanced up to find him watching her with a strange intensity, something beyond the desire that usually made him so focused. It was like he was *looking* for something inside of her. Something hidden.

"May I ask you something?" he said, his voice soft and rough in the quiet room.

She hesitated, taken aback by his request for permission. And even more stunned by her own desire to answer whatever he asked. As if she could be open with him.

It was amazing how easily pleasure could erode walls, making it seem that a connection had been made when it hadn't. It couldn't. Not again.

"You and I both know that I cannot say no," she said, reminding them both of their situation.

His mouth turned down, but he shook his head. "You cannot say no to my sexual demands. But you could always refuse to tell me what I want to hear. Or lie."

Lie. The word hung between them like a slap. That was what he thought of her, after all. That she was a liar, that she had played him for a fool over and over. Nathan had always been willing to believe the very worst of her.

She sighed. "What do you want to know?"

"Your parents, what do they think of what you do in London?" He continued to look at her intently.

Cassandra jolted. Indeed, he had struck upon a topic she never expected. Her mother had been the governess of one of Nathan's childhood friends, and her father had tailored a few items for his father. He had only met them a handful of times, and only once after they struck up the affair that had led them to this.

Her parents, like his, had not approved, fearing the censure she would face if she entered Nathan's world. They had been just as vocal as his father and mother, although less insulting. And far less willing to do whatever it took to stop them from marrying.

"Cass?" he said softly.

She melted. In the heat of passion, the endearment of her shortened name could be explained away, but now he was rational again. He had to know what using her nickname meant to her when he said it so softly.

Did he even realize he used it, or was it an intentional manipulation?

She shrugged. "They are proud of my success as a seamstress," she said quietly. "My father especially, as he taught me that trade."

"What of the other things?" he pressed, voice low. "The other business, the fact that you have been a mistress during your years here?"

Cassandra sat up a fraction, staring at him. "Why do you want to know?"

He shook his head slightly. "I just wondered. I know your father was quite ill last year and that you send a good deal of money home to them monthly. I wondered if they ever question how you have so much to share."

She pushed off the couch and turned to stare at him fully. She ached as his body parted from hers, but she was too upset to feel the full extent of the sting of separation.

"How do you know those things?" she barked, hearing the wild tone to her voice even as she tried to control it.

He seemed surprised by her reaction and sat up, facing her in all his naked, muscular glory.

"I . . . I kept an eye on things," he admitted.

She stumbled back, her hand lifting to her mouth. "From the moment you came to me with your threats, I realized you had me followed, watched, *spied* upon. It was the only way you could have known so much," she whispered, proud that she was reining in control when she was shaking so hard. "But you did the same to my family?"

"Cassand—"

She cut him off. "Were you trying to find more ways to blackmail and hurt me? Trying to uncover some kind of secrets about them to hold over my head in case my own didn't suffice?"

He was up on his feet then, his hands held out in mute entreaty. "No! I never would have brought them into this. I just knew how close you were . . . you are. And I wondered—"

"Or maybe you just wanted to keep them as extra leverage to hold over my head. You asked me what they thought, you made comments about my father's illness . . ." She was livid now, her hands shaking out of control, her stomach rolling with nausea. "If I don't bend to your will even further, do you plan to tell them that I am a whore and a sex monger?"

His lips pursed, but he didn't reply.

His silence was all she needed. "You bastard."

She spun away, grabbing for her discarded clothing as her breath came in heaves.

"That isn't it at all," he snapped, coming within reach and extending his hand toward her.

She lurched away, their beautiful joining damaged, broken, by her new fears.

"It is one thing to blackmail me with the end of my reputation and livelihood," she said softly, finally meeting his eyes. "But if you intended to hurt my family, then you are so far gone that the boy I knew, the man I wanted to marry, the man

I—" she stopped herself. "Well, he is gone. Maybe he never existed."

She headed for the door and for once Nathan didn't stalk after her. He merely watched, an almost stricken expression on his face.

She didn't look back, she didn't have the strength. At the door, she paused. "I know you'll be back. I will be ready. The sooner you can purge whatever twisted ill will you have toward me, the sooner we can both move on with our lives as if none of this ever happened, the better."

And for the first time, as she left the room and hurried up the stairs, she meant every word.

Chapter Nine

*W*hen the missive came demanding that she meet with the Marquis of Herstale, Cassandra wasn't surprised. Although she had not spoken to or even seen the man in years, she had been waiting for this moment since she saw Nathan again in his aunt's home.

Nathan's father had always been driven to keep them apart. There was no reason to assume it would be any different now, despite the years, and despite the heartache the man's last attempts had brought to them both.

Her first reaction was to refuse. Or ignore the note. Or to run away from London entirely and forget that Nathan and his family had barged, uninvited, back into her life. But in the end, none of those actions would do her any good in the long run. The Marquis would pursue her until he had his say.

And Nathan . . . well, although Nathan had not called upon her or contacted her in three days since their last encounter, he was only biding his time. Her heart told her that he wasn't finished with her yet. If she ran, he would follow her and the situation would only be worse in the end.

So she sent a note back to the Marquis, telling his lordship to expect her call that afternoon.

And now she stood in the middle of a parlor in one of the biggest homes in London, staring at the gold-encrusted clock that sat ticking on the mantel of a ridiculously large fireplace. It said that she had been waiting for more than half an hour.

She shifted in annoyance, brought back to a similar scene in the country years ago. The Marquis had tried to buy her away from Nathan. When that hadn't worked, he had threatened and eventually shouted. But she had been so sure of Nathan's love, so devoted to her own for him, that she hadn't been moved. She hadn't known what her refusal of the Marquis' offer would unleash. Or ultimately reveal about Nathan's true feelings.

The door to the parlor opened and she turned to face the man who had been her silent nemesis her entire adult life. When he entered the room, she drew in a sucking gasp of breath.

Although only a handful of years separated them from that ugly day in another parlor, the Marquis had aged a decade or more. His salted dark hair was now almost entirely gray, and his broad shoulders and muscles had been eaten down by illness, making him smaller and far less imposing. And he walked with the help of a cane that he leaned most of his weight upon as he passed by the servant who had opened the door for him.

He waved the man off and the door shut behind him. Only then did Cassandra see the powerful lord she remembered. He was still alive in the Marquis' hawkish blue eyes. The ones his son had inherited.

She shivered despite herself.

"We had a deal," the old man said, his voice in no way as weak as his body.

Cassandra folded her arms. Although he remained imposing, she was not the same terrified girl she had been that long-ago afternoon. She refused to let him bully her. Or make her feel small and worthless.

Those days were long gone.

"Good day to you, too, my lord," she said softly, feigning just the right touch of boredom as evidenced by the light of frustration that entered his eyes. "It has been a long time."

"Not long enough in my estimation, Miss Willows," the Marquis said, as he creaked forward, step by slow step.

"Nor mine." She met his gaze solidly. That seemed to surprise him, for he stopped advancing and merely tilted his head to the side. It was as if he hadn't fully recognized her until now, or perhaps he was finally realizing that she had changed on the inside as much as he had externally. Where he had lost his strength, she had found hers. They were on far more equal ground now.

"I offered you money, Miss Willows. You took that money. And now I hear that you have met more than once with my son." He arched one graying brow. "How can that be?"

Cassandra had spent a great deal of time releasing her anger. She had come to accept the past, mourn it and move on. She realized that hating the Marquis, hating what he had done, hating Nathan for his lack of faith . . . those things only served to hurt her.

Yet, his lordship's question, his pointed statement about the distasteful bond they shared, awoke the emotions she had long believed dead. And the anger she had so long stifled burned hot in her belly as she stared at him.

"If you recall, my lord, the payment you gave me was a form of recompense for what *your* actions caused. There was nothing about Nathan in that bargain."

She couldn't help but smile when the man flinched and broke his gaze away from hers. So he still felt shame for his actions. Good. She hoped it haunted him every day.

The Marquis flexed his fingers against his cane. The grip was shaped like a serpent's head and Cassandra barely resisted the urge to laugh at the irony.

"You know I do not want you to see him. To confuse him. He is finally back where he belongs and then you pursue him!"

Cassandra shook her head. "You should pay for better spies, my lord. Your son came to me. I would have been happy to stay away."

Except that wasn't true. If he hadn't come to her, she would have been eaten at by emptiness. Perhaps she would have pursued him at that point. Seduced him. But the Marquis didn't have to know that.

The older man's nostrils flared. "My son came to you?"

She nodded. "There is much you do not know about him. And clearly much he does not realize about you, sir."

Now the Marquis advanced again, much faster than before, though it seemed he paid for it when his breath grew short and labored.

"It was better for him not to know!" he blurted out between puffs of painful sounding air.

Cassandra shrugged. "Perhaps. Perhaps not."

The old man was livid now, his pale hands shaking and his eyes wide and wild with anger, but also with fear. "If you think you can hold our bargain over my head, or get more money out of me—"

"In case you haven't heard, I don't need your money," Cassandra interrupted with a dismissive wave of her hand. "And even if I did, I would *never* tell Nathan about our bargain. About the reason behind it."

The Marquis turned his head to the side, again examining her like she was some kind of strange specimen of a creature he had never seen before. But of course he wouldn't understand. He certainly had no compassion or kindness. At least none she had ever seen, though his son was loyal enough that she guessed he had exhibited such emotions at some time in his decrepit life.

"Why wouldn't you tell him," the Marquis asked, "if you know the trouble it could bring me?"

Cassandra balked at the question. Her anger, which had reached the boiling point when the man entered the room, faded as she thought of Nathan.

"I don't keep the secret for you, old man, that is for certain," she said softly. Then she turned and stared across the room toward a bright, sunlit window. "I keep my counsel because, as you say, it is better for Nathan not to know. If he did, it might destroy him. And I would not do such a thing willingly, no matter what has transpired between us."

She turned back to the Marquis. In the end, he was just a withered old man who had sold his soul to "protect" his son from someone who wanted nothing more than to love him. And if his appearance was any judge, living with his guilt had brought him enough pain.

"If this is the only subject of our meeting, I shall go," Cassandra said softly. "Please do not call on me again, my lord, for I will not come at your insistence. Good day."

She brushed past him and moved for the door, desperate to get out of this house, out of the company of this man who brought back such trying memories.

"Miss Willows."

She hesitated as she reached for the door, drawing in an exasperated breath before she turned back. "Yes, my lord?"

The Marquis leaned heavily on his cane with both hands now, as exhausted by this meeting as she was. He sighed before he met her eyes and for the first time she didn't feel his distain and judgment of her stature in life.

"Perhaps Nathan did come to you, but you have the power

to send him away. It is best for all involved if you do so. You cannot have him."

She stared at the shell of a man who had once been so vibrant. And she thought of the angry, vengeful shell that Nathan inhabited now. He was but a husk of the loving, laughing man she had known before. Both of them made her so desperately sad.

"I am more than well aware that we cannot have each other, my lord. Not for long."

Then she exited the room without asking his leave.

Nathan stared out the window of the rolling carriage, watching the twinkling lights of the city pass by. Every jolt and bump moved him closer to home and farther away from his evening at a club where he drank too much and thought even more.

His head was spinning from whiskey and blurry, powerful images of Cassandra.

When he told her he planned to blackmail her, he'd thought it would make it easier to get over her. It was a way to have her, use her, then discard her like she had done to him all those years ago.

But now . . . things had grown complicated. As hard as he tried, he was not capable of turning off his emotions when he touched her. Nor could he hold on to his anger or really do anything except luxuriate in the grip of her body as he entered her and reveled in her moans of pleasure.

The vehicle stopped in front of his London townhome and

Nathan slowly departed the carriage and staggered up the walkway. He hardly acknowledged his butler as he trudged through the door. What he needed now was his bed and a deep sleep, hopefully devoid of dreams of Cassandra thanks to the alcohol coursing through his system.

Moving up the stairs, he thought of their final moments the last time they'd been together. She had all but accused him of threatening her family, and he supposed he couldn't blame her for that. After all, he had resorted to blackmail already and he had brought her mother and father into the conversation. Why wouldn't she link the two things?

The truth was, as much as he wanted to return the hurt Cassandra had brought down on him, he did have his limits. Hurting her family, destroying their view of her, making her an outcast with the people she loved . . . those were apparently his limits.

But *she* didn't know that, and somehow that stung. He didn't trust her, and he certainly had done nothing to earn her trust in return, but damn, how he wished she knew he hadn't sunk that low. That he wouldn't.

He pushed his chamber door open and entered the darkened room. Sometime during the night, his valet had come in and lit a few candles and fed the fire, but after the brighter glow of the hallways, it took a moment for his eyes to adjust.

When they did, he staggered back in surprise, hitting the door with his shoulder and forcing it shut with a slam.

There, lying across his bed with her head propped up on her hand was Cassandra.

He blinked a few times. He'd had more than a few drinks, was he hallucinating?

"Cassandra?" he croaked.

She didn't reply, but merely pushed from the bed to her feet. He sucked in a harsh breath. She was wearing the most delightful concoction of sheer fabric that he'd ever seen. Black as the night outside, but still translucent enough that her body was clearly outlined beneath. And it was shockingly short, just barely skimming over the middle of her thighs so that her long, pale legs were bare.

"How are you here?" he asked, his voice shaking from surprise and need.

She moved closer, the shadows obscuring her expression. "It is amazing what one can do and where one can go when one pays the right servants."

He cocked his head, amazed she would resort to bribery when all she had to do was send him word. God knew he was unable to resist her. If she had actually instigated a meeting . . .

"*Why* are you here?" he asked.

She reached him and the light hit her face. She was smiling, but it wasn't an expression of kindness or joy. There was a hard edge to it. A hint of . . . anger. Bitterness.

"Why do you think, Nathan?" she asked, her tone matching her expression. Then the smile fell away entirely. "No one tells me what to do. Not anymore."

Nathan's eyebrows knit together in confusion. Was she trying to regain control over this situation by initiating this encounter? He stared at her, so beautiful in her revealing garment, her pink nipples swollen under the sheer fabric, the musky, hot smell of her sex already wafting up to him and making him mad with lust.

But did he want her like this? When anger and desperation were her driving forces?

He opened his mouth to argue that point with her, but she didn't allow it. She latched her arms around his neck and then her mouth crushed to his with angry, heated passion. A passion he couldn't deny no matter how many rational arguments he made with himself about her motives. The moment he tasted her kiss, the moment her hot body molded to his, he was lost.

And he wanted to claim her in an elemental way. To burn his imprint on her so that she wouldn't be able to forget that he had taken her. Even when he was married to another and she had a new lover.

The kiss shifted in that moment. She had been dominating it, but now he took over, slanting his mouth over his for greater access and reveling in her deep, needy moan that was lost in his mouth.

But then she shook away from him, backing up.

"I want you now," she said, moving toward the bed. She motioned to where she had been lying and he saw for the first time the pile of toys she had brought with her.

His eyes widened when he recognized the velvety restraints and the glass dildo they had played with before. His body clenched at the memory. But in addition to those things were clamps of some kind, a blindfold, and a filmy liquid in a small vial. The assortment of accoutrements was unexpected and, yes, highly arousing, but also confusing.

"Like this?" he asked, motioning to the group of items.

She nodded and swept up the little clips. Moving toward him, she whispered, "These are for my nipples. Put them on and they will ache with the need to be touched. Only you can set me free from that ache."

His eyes widened. Her voice was so husky, so dark and sensual. She had never spoken to him like that before. She was no longer Cassandra, the girl he'd once known. Now she was Cassandra, the mistress moaning to her protector. She was a sex goddess made to seduce and pleasure.

But when he looked into her eyes, he still sensed a distance there. But he could get her back. He had forced that connection before, he was driven to do it again.

Reaching out, he glided the flimsy straps of her lingerie down her shoulders, baring her breasts in the shimmering candlelight. She was already on the edge, he could sense it in the way she shivered when the fine, silky fabric caressed her already hard nipples.

He couldn't wait to see what she would do as he took the clamps from her trembling fingers. He looked at them carefully. Although they were made to pinch, they didn't seem to be cruel. He opened one and fitted it around the hard, pink swell of one nipple. As he closed it, Cassandra let out a whimper of pleasure and her eyes fluttered shut.

"The other one," she ordered without looking at him.

He followed her directive, sliding the second clip into place. As soon as he closed the mechanism, Cassandra let out a soft cry. Her hands clutched his shoulders and she shook, eyes squeezed shut and legs trembling.

His eyes widened. She was coming, orgasming just from the focused tug on her breasts. Of course she had always been exquisitely sensitive there. He'd never known a woman before or since who got so much pleasure from a lick or squeeze of her nipple.

He was rock hard by that point, his cock swelling against the front of his trousers and rubbing uncomfortably against the fastenings.

"What else?" she asked, her tone breathless as she came down from the orgasm. "What else do you want? To tie me up again? To make me helpless with an aphrodisiac?"

He stared at the vial. So that's what it was. He had heard of such things in India that were used in some brothels to make the women wild and insatiable. But he didn't want Cassandra that way. Not out of her mind with lust for any man.

Just for him. And from his touch, not because a drug was addling her mind and making her do what she might not consider under other circumstances.

He shook his head. "No drug."

She tilted her head. "You want to use me, don't you?" she cooed, but again there was no softness to her demeanor. "You want to vent your anger. So how will you do it, Nathan? How will you do it tonight?"

He flinched. She wasn't speaking anything but the truth,

but to hear it couched in such plain terms made him feel even more like a cad than he already had before.

"No," he muttered, backing a step away from her and holding up his hands in a gesture of surrender. "Not like this. Not when I'm drunk and you're so filled with rage that you're practically quivering."

She shook her head. "Why not? You've been filled with equal rage and fucked me. And it was good. So why can't I have what I want?"

Her fingers snaked down and she cupped his cock through his trousers, squeezing with just the right amount of tension to make his knees buckle and a groan escape his lips.

"And you want me. So why care what the reasons are? Why think about anything else but having each other?"

Before he could answer, she dropped down to her knees before him and with deft, experienced fingers she opened his trousers and let them fall around his ankles.

His erection sprang free, thrusting up in silent demand for her body, even as he tried to resist her with his mind. But at that moment, still spinning with drink and surprise, he couldn't resist the pull of pleasure. Especially when Cassandra stroked the hard, heavy length of him with her palm and then wrapped her ruby lips around his cock, sucking him deep into her throat with a muffled moan of pleasure.

"Christ," he managed to grind out through clenched teeth. He clutched at her shoulders, catching some of her hair with his fingers and causing it to tumble down around her bare back in a fragrant cloud.

She didn't hesitate, pounding her mouth around him, sucking him deeper on each thrust and working the base of his cock with her hand as she withdrew. She had done this before, just a few days earlier. But that night it had felt like a gift. Now it was something different.

But damn if it wasn't good.

In quick order, Nathan's vision began to blur, his hands and legs shook, his cock was on fire, the intensity of pleasure so great that it bordered on pain. He sensed the impending explosion, felt his seed moving from deep within him. He jerked to pull away, but she held tight, continuing to suck and work at him until he couldn't hold back any longer and he came.

She took it all, every ounce, looking up at him as she did it with a challenging light to her eyes. She had done this, she had conquered him, it was clear that was how she felt.

Only, as his breathing returned to normal and his body stopped twitching and shaking from the power of his orgasm, he knew it wasn't over. This was war, after all, and he wasn't about to surrender with just one skirmish.

She pulled away, wiping her mouth with the back of her hand as she pulled the negligee straps up her arms to cover her breasts. He caught her hands before she could finish the action.

"Where do you think you're going?" he asked, dragging her back against him so that the soft clips around her nipples rubbed across his jacket. Her hips bucked, but her gaze never left his.

"Home," she all but snarled. "I've done what I came here to do."

"No." Without finesse, he thrust her backward, letting her fall across the settee, her legs splayed perfectly for his plans. "Now it's my turn."

Chapter Ten

Cassandra's eyes widened as she stared up at Nathan from her splayed position on the settee.

"Nath—"

She didn't get a chance to finish saying his name. Her voice instead transformed into a loud, needy moan when he brought his mouth down between her legs. He spread her wide, the translucent silk of her negligee straining against her pussy as he licked across her wet slit and pressed the fabric against her swollen clit.

"Turnabout is fair play," he panted against her skin and her hips bucked up as his breath heated her sensitive flesh.

She tried not to be moved by Nathan's touch, but it was impossible when he was pushing the wet fabric that separated them away and driving his tongue into her slick entrance. He groaned against her flesh like he couldn't get enough of her taste, her scent.

She had come here to prove something to herself, to prove something to him, to make him come and regain control, to forget that his father had, once again, tried to keep her from this pleasure.

But now the tables were turned. Her anger, her indignation, and her drive to prove something were all fading away, replaced instead with the most intense pleasure she had ever felt. Nathan was using his whole mouth to pleasure her, sucking her swollen flesh between his lips, lapping at every inch of her sex, and even scraping his teeth over her clit until tears streamed down her face and she bit her lip almost bloody to keep from begging for more.

His fingers joined in on the torment now. With his index and middle fingers he stroked deep inside of her clenching, trembling body, curling the digits upward until he hit upon the hidden bundle of nerves deep within her. When he began to suck her clit in time with the motion of his fingers, she lost all control.

Pleasure and release hit her like a punch, stealing her breath, robbing her of coherent words and thoughts. All she could do was scream, her throat throbbing, her lungs constricting while wave after wave of impossible pleasure shook her.

He was relentless, dragging her through the pleasure, forcing her to feel more and more and more of it until she was lying weak against the settee cushions. Until her legs ached from trembling. Until her sheath was soaked and tender from coming.

Finally, he lifted his head and removed his fingers from her body gently. Fire burned in his bright eyes and when Cassandra was able to find the strength to sit up, she saw that his cock was hard as steel and ready again.

The outrageous desire that he had only just slaked returned with a terrifying speed and power. She had brought the aphrodisiac along with her tonight in case he wanted to use it, but Nathan didn't need a drug to make her insatiable.

He did that all on his own.

She grasped his cheeks and kissed him, driving her tongue into his mouth, tasting her own body on him. God, it drove her wild. *He* drove her wild. Even if she hated herself for it, he was the best sex she'd ever had. The only man who could make her ache until she sobbed, lose control and beg for more.

But tonight she had to finish this without begging. When he rose up, bracing his arms on either side of her head as he met the strokes of her tongue with hard, harsh thrusts of his own, she fought to keep her mind in the present.

"Sit," she ordered between kisses, pushing him away to sit on the settee cushions.

He followed the order, though he could have easily kept her on her back and taken her without any trouble.

"Still at war?" he asked, watching her through unreadable eyes as she crawled to her knees and then straddled his lap.

"Oh, Nathan," she practically purred as she fitted herself over the hot thrust of his cock. "You and I will always be at war. Why not just surrender?"

In response, he lifted his hips and entered her in one smooth stroke. Cassandra couldn't help her cry of pleasure as he filled her, stretched her, and made her aching body throb even more acutely.

She clutched at his shoulders, digging her nails in as they grappled for control. She thrust down on him hard, rubbing her hips against him so that her clit stroked against his pelvis. But he wasn't ready to give over ground. Each time she pushed down over him, he lifted his hips, hitting that sweet spot inside of her that made her head roll back and her lips utter incoherent moans of pleasure.

Their bodies writhed together, finally finding a rhythm where neither one gave ground, where each tormented the other. They were equals in the pleasure—until Nathan reached up and unclipped the clamps around her nipples. Cassandra yelped in surprise as blood rushed back to the sensitive peaks. And they *were* exquisitely sensitive now, so that even the brush of the air against them made her tremble.

So when Nathan sucked one hard peak into his mouth, swirling his tongue around the aching nipple, she was lost. The orgasm hit her so hard that she almost lost consciousness. He cupped her backside as her hips careened out of control. When all she could do was buck helplessly, he worked his cock into her from below as he sucked, and pleasured, and teased both nipples until they were on fire.

And then he took advantage of her weakened state by flipping her over on her back across the bed. She arched beneath him as he whispered, "War, my sweet."

He cupped her knee, crooking it high over his shoulder, and thrust into her. He was hard, he was fast, and he was magnificent. Her clenching body squeezed on as her orgasm dragged out further and further.

But finally he took mercy on her. Or perhaps he simply lost control himself. His smooth strokes grew as erratic as her own wild hips, and his focused torment of her raw body ended. The veins in his neck began to strain, his eyes squeezed shut, and with a curse, he came, the hot splash of his seed heating her body as he filled her.

Nathan could hardly breathe as he reveled in the pleasure of just being inside her body. The closeness of having her wrapped around him as he found pleasure. He had promised himself he wouldn't do that ever again, but now that he had, he remembered how damned addictive it could be.

Shifting to his side, he wrapped his arms around her and held her to his chest with a contented sigh. But to his surprise, Cassandra didn't relax against him with the same sated pleasure. Her spine remained stiff as she turned her face away from his.

Leaning away, he looked down into her eyes and frowned. The distance he had sensed in her earlier remained. If anything, in the afterglow she seemed more far away, angrier. Even though she had experienced pleasure. Even though their war was over.

Wasn't it?

Right now it didn't seem to be.

"Are you finished with me for the night, then?" she asked, her cold voice shattering the warmth he had felt until that moment.

He frowned, hating how she refused to meet his gaze. Hating how she could convince herself that what had just happened meant nothing. Hating that he feared perhaps making love *didn't* actually signify to her in any way.

"No," he said, low and dangerous. "Cassandra you cannot pretend this away."

"There is nothing to pretend," she said, pulling back from him. He still had his arms around her and held her easily. "I came here. We fucked, just as I agreed to do. Why make it anything more than what it is?"

Nathan flinched at the dismissiveness to her tone. She was all the distant mistress now. Not a woman who craved a man, but one who came to him for what he could give. Or what he could save her from.

She tugged at his arms, but he refused to let her up. The moment she broke the contact of their bodies she could fully convince herself that she had only come to him out of some fulfillment of their bargain—not because she wanted him, not because she needed this. And he wanted to make her remember that she did need him, for as long as he could.

Her eyes widened as she struggled.

"Let me go," she said, and now there was a hint of alarm in her tone.

He shook his head. "You can't escape me so easily, Cas-sandra. You can't put distance between what you wanted and what you did. Not without facing a fight from me."

She struggled harder. "Please!"

"You came here because you craved me with the same power I crave you. Don't pretend otherwise."

"Nathan!"

Her tone was so sharp and her struggles had become so wild that Nathan released her in surprise. Cassandra bolted away, grabbing her clothing as she moved. She held them up to cover her as she faced him.

Nathan stared, all thoughts of forcing Cassandra to see the hypocrisy of her denials long gone. She was shaking like a leaf, obviously filled with real fear. Her eyes were wide and wild as she dressed, but she never took their pain-filled stare away from him. Like an animal watching a hunter in the forest, aware that he might strike at any moment.

"What is wrong with you?" he asked, getting to his feet without bothering to cover himself. "Is this display some kind of game?"

She shook her head, but her trembling continued. "No games, Nathan. Please . . . please just let me go. Let me go."

With that, she spun away and all but ran from the room, leaving behind her hairpins, her toys, and the scent of her skin as she fled. Nathan stared at her retreating form and con-tinued to stare at the open door in shock long after she had gone.

Tonight had been a war, a sensual battle of wits that he had enjoyed at every moment. Until the last. Because when he felt the wall between them, the chasm of distance that Cassandra still held, he had to admit that he didn't like it.

But there was more than that to make him wonder, worry. He had never seen Cassandra so . . . *afraid* as when he used his strength to control her. Even though he would never hurt her. Or force her to do anything against her will. But it was as if in that charged, emotional moment, she had forgotten that.

Forgotten his character. Or never really known it at all.

And it left him wondering what secrets she kept inside. What had happened that would make her bolt like a frightened rabbit, especially after she had come to him like a sexual warrior? He didn't know. But he was sure as hell going to find out, even if it meant doing the one thing he would surely regret because it would only cause him trouble. So much more trouble than he already faced as this twisted bargain between he and Cassandra stretched on and on and on.

Cassandra sat in her darkened carriage, trembling in the cold as she made her way home. She had left her wrap at Nathan's home. That and about half her other things. Because she had run away. What satisfaction that must give him, to see her bolt. How he must be laughing to know how much he could control her.

Except, when she finally broke free of his grip, he had looked anything but amused or satisfied. He had seemed confused. Even . . . *worried*.

She shook her head, trying to clear her mind of the memories that had been stirred there when he held her in place. Ugly images flooded her mind.

Pain. Fear. Humiliation.

"No!"

She said the word out loud and the sound brought her back to the present. She wasn't in that terrifying place. She was in her very nice carriage, going to her very nice home. A safe haven.

From the ashes of that fear and pain and humiliation, she had built a life of her own making. She had become powerful in her own way. She had chosen her path. Until Nathan returned and stole that power and control away. Even tonight, when she had come at him with every intention of making him come and then leaving him alone to stew on how easily she could manage it, in the end she had been the one to surrender.

She straightened her spine as the carriage rolled to a stop at her pretty townhome. Nathan could too easily make her forget their shared past and her vows to never again let a man control her heart. She couldn't allow it, not ever again.

Not ever again. She had to end this before he wrapped her into his world and she lost everything she'd worked so hard and suffered so greatly to obtain.

Chapter Eleven

Nathan rubbed his temples as the incessant noise went on and on around him, filling his mind with ceaseless chatter, making his ears ring with empty words. How could three women talk so endlessly about bonnets?

He looked up with a weak smile as his aunt thumped her hand on the arm of her chair and snapped, "Nathan!"

"Yes, Aunt Bethany?"

"You seem distracted, are we boring you?" She eyed him with a look of complete mischief and Nathan's eyes widened. The old bat was *enjoying* tormenting him, after all. He almost laughed at the realization.

"Of course not, Aunt," he said with an innocent tilt of the head. "In fact, all this talk about clothing and bonnets has put me to mind of a wonderful idea."

"What's that, Nathan?" his sister Lydia asked, taking a dainty sip of her tea. At nineteen and in her second season, Lydia was still mindful of everything she did and said. Nathan had caught her practicing her responses to being asked to dance more than once.

Unlike his other sister, Adelaide. Though she was just a year older than Lydia, she had much more experience with the world of the *ton*. In fact, she had refused one proposal already, much to the chagrin of their mother.

"Yes, do tell what could have possibly interested you about bonnets," Adelaide said with a light laugh.

"The last time I was here, Aunt Bethany had a guest, if you recall."

Nathan swallowed, trying not to remember in full detail his reaction when he had seen Cassandra for the first time in so long. How much anger, pain, and pure desire had coursed through him. *Still* ripped through his veins like acid whenever he was near her.

"A seamstress, I believe," he continued, measuring his tone and expression carefully so that none of the women would recognize how bloody important this was to him. "Miss Willows, I think her name is?"

His aunt nodded enthusiastically. "Yes! Best *modiste* in London by far, that one."

"And Mama refuses to allow us to have a gown from her," Lydia said with a pout.

Nathan couldn't have asked for a better opening. "Yes, I recall that. I also recall how much you two seemed to desire such a gown from the lady. Since I have returned, you have both been such good and caring sisters—"

"Because we have missed you so terribly, Nathan," Adelaide interrupted, pressing his hand briefly with her own.

He smiled and it was not forced. "And I missed the two of you. To show my gratitude, I thought perhaps *I* could arrange for a gown to be made, one for each of you, by Miss Willows. So as to not upset Mother, perhaps you would allow the seamstress to do her fittings here, Aunt?"

As his sisters let out twin squeals of delight and started chattering to each other and singing his praises, all without drawing breath, Nathan waited. If his aunt wouldn't agree to Cassandra working here, this would never work. His mother certainly wouldn't invite his lover into her home. And somehow he doubted that Cassandra would wish to go there and face the two people who had spoken out so passionately against her all those years ago.

His aunt eyed him for a long moment, her hawkish gaze piercing so fully that he feared she might have guessed his deeper connection with Cassandra. But finally she shrugged one slender shoulder.

"I don't see that as a problem. I think it's ridiculous that your mother refuses to use Cassandra Willows. I must keep needling her reason out of her."

Nathan shut his eyes briefly. God, if his aunt ever *did* uncover the truth, that would be a nightmare in itself.

"I can't speak to that, I'm afraid," he murmured, avoiding the direct lie as carefully as he could. His aunt might pick up on any deception, she had always been good at that. "But I assume from all your screaming and jumping that you girls would be amenable to the idea of having Miss Willows make dresses for you?"

His sisters lunged toward him in tandem, nearly knocking him down as they hugged him, chattering at once about silks and satins and waistlines.

"Good," he said with a laugh, as they finally released him from their surprisingly strong grips and returned to their seats to put their heads together and giggle. "Though I would recommend we don't tell Mother until your gowns are finished."

The girls nodded their heads, as did his aunt.

"Aunt Bethany, could you contact the lady?"

His aunt looked up at him with renewed surprise. "I gave you her direction a few weeks ago, did I not? I assumed you had already made some kind of contact and arrangement with her."

Nathan bit back a curse. She *had* passed along Cassandra's information to him, hadn't she? Well, there was no way to tell her that he had used it to blackmail Cassandra into his bed rather than to discuss fine satin with her. So he shrugged.

"I'm afraid I misplaced the card in all the excitement of the last few weeks. And I think since you two already have a working relationship of sorts that she might be more open to a sudden request for a fitting from you rather than from a man she . . ."

He hesitated. He couldn't exactly say "didn't know" or "hadn't met," could he?

"Yes, yes, I suppose you are correct," his aunt said with a fluttering, dismissive wave of her hand. "I will send word to Miss Willows directly and let you know when she will meet with the girls here."

Nathan nodded, filled with relief. But as the women returned to their talking, he paced to the window to look out on the street below. His plans for Cassandra were coming together now. Now he could only hope that she would accept his aunt's request.

Cassandra trudged up the stairs to Lady Bethany Worthington's home, her shoulders rolled forward and her steps sloppy. As much as she tried to deny and hide it, her exhaustion was overwhelming.

Since the last time she and Nathan had been together, she had hardly slept. Four long nights of working until her fingers ached . . . and then tossing and turning in her cold bed while she thought of Nathan. The war between them for control. But mostly she thought of their renewed passion. Somehow she hadn't thought the connection to him could be deeper or more powerful than it had been years ago when she first loved him.

But it was. Time had altered them both and now the passion was deeper, the emotion sharper.

It was dangerous. She didn't want it, and she had to find a way to stop wanting him, but judging from his avoidance of her ever since she ran away from him, perhaps that wouldn't be an issue anymore. Of course, every time she began to believe she was free, Nathan found a way to barge back into her life.

At the door, she stood up a bit straighter and smoothed her gown carefully. She had been surprised to be summoned to Lady Worthington's home, but unable to refuse. Nathan's aunt was too powerful and influential a lady to ignore. She only hoped the woman wouldn't want to talk about her nephew and his pursuit of a bride while Cassandra measured her. There was a great deal she could take, but today that topic was not one she cared to broach.

The door opened after she knocked, revealing Lady Worthington's tall, stern butler. The man didn't speak as Cassandra gave her name, but merely motioned her down the hallway toward the parlor where Cassandra could hear Lady Worthington talking to someone.

Wonderful, the old bat had company. That only increased the possibility that Nathan would be a subject of conversation. From what Cassandra had gleaned from other clients, the man was the talk of London, with everyone desperate to know when he would take a bride and who the lucky lady might be.

As the butler announced her, Cassandra did her best to put a bright smile on her face. Lady Worthington was sharp enough that she might notice Cassandra's tiredness and demand an explanation. Or worse, spread news of it around town and possibly limit her clients.

"Come in, my dear," Lady Worthington said in that sharp-as-a-knife tone of hers that left no room for refusal. "You are late."

Cassandra tilted her head in deference as she entered the room. "I do apologize, my lady. I'm afraid I lost track of time while working on a . . ."

She stopped. What she had been working on that morning was a highly polished set of sensual balls that could be slipped inside a woman's body for pleasure and to build the inner muscles of her sheath. Not exactly a fact she could share with Lady Worthington.

"On a project," she finally finished with a vague wave of her hand.

"Hmph." Lady Worthington motioned behind Cassandra. "Have you met my great-nieces?"

Cassandra stilled before she slowly turned and faced the two girls who were perched on the settee behind her.

Great God, Nathan's sisters.

The girls had been young when she and Nathan had carried on their affair and she had only glimpsed them from afar once while riding with their brother. Now they were young women, both in the bloom of their beauty. Both with Nathan's bright blue eyes.

Cassandra almost choked, but managed to remain calm.

"Lady Adelaide and Lady Lydia, I believe?" she said, pretending to search for their names when in reality they were right on her lips.

The girls leaped up and both began talking at once. They praised her designs and even complimented her on the pretty dress she was wearing. Cassandra smiled and this time it wasn't forced. There was no denying the fresh, innocent charm of the sisters. They flattered her with their kindness, but she was full-aware that all that would likely fade away if the two young women realized what kind of relationship she had once shared with their exalted brother. Or the one she shared with him now.

The kindness of the *ton* only stretched so far as long as one stayed in one's place. Dare to reach for more and all the sweetness and friendliness would vanish in an instant. She had learned that the hard way, most certainly.

"Girls!" Lady Worthington snapped, and the two fell instantly silent.

Cassandra turned back to their aunt, who was rolling her eyes at their girlish excitement. She couldn't help but smother a laugh. Lady Worthington might be a terrifying old woman, but she was also direct and quite enjoyable. Cassandra actually looked forward to the day when she was advanced enough in age and settled enough in fortune that she could do whatever she damned well pleased. Lady Worthington was certainly an excellent role model for such a life.

"What is it that I can do for you, Lady Worthington?" she said through her laughter.

"Not for me, my dear, though I am so looking forward to seeing my gown."

Cassandra nodded. "I will have it finished in three days' time and bring it by for you the afternoon of the twelfth, if that is satisfactory."

"Perfect!" The older woman clasped her hands together.

"And perhaps, if you work very quickly, you could also bring two more gowns with you at the same time."

Cassandra couldn't help it. Her smile fell and she swallowed reflexively. God, two more gowns? She was already overrun as it was.

"Two more?" she repeated, her voice weak.

Lady Worthington tilted her head as if she heard Cassandra's exhaustion, but continued on, "I asked you here today because someone would like for you to make a gown for each of my nieces."

Cassandra tossed a look at the excited girls and then back to Lady Worthington in confusion. "*Someone*?"

It sure as hell wasn't their parents. Lord and Lady Herstale had made it perfectly clear that they thought Cassandra was worth less than the dirt on their shoes.

Suddenly, the realization of the truth hit her and Cassandra found herself reaching for the back of the nearest chair to keep herself upright. As if on cue, Nathan strode through the door, a secretive smile on his handsome face. He bent to kiss his aunt's cheek.

"So sorry I was late, Aunt, I got caught up in a conversation with Lord Smythe-Gray at the club. A windbag, that one," he said.

His aunt smiled indulgently. "A windbag who is angling for you to court his daughter."

For the first time, Nathan shot a brief, almost apologetic look her way, but Cassandra forced herself to turn her head. She fought her jealousy. After all, she was fully aware that Nathan was on the lookout for a bride. A "proper" one, as he had sneered at her only a few weeks ago. Cassandra had designed a very beautiful dress for Lady Eliza Smythe-Gray a few weeks ago and had found her to be everything a lady should be.

Everything Cassandra was not.

The very pretty girl would certainly make a fine Countess for him. The sooner Nathan found his bride, the sooner he would end his pursuit of her. She was happy if he was courting. And eventually her heart would accept what her head already knew, she was certain.

"Hello Lydia, Adelaide," he said around Cassandra, ignoring his aunt's comment about the apparent designs of Lord Smythe-Gray.

The girls said their hellos in unison and Nathan shook his head with a kind smile that touched Cassandra's heart. He had always loved his younger siblings. It seemed that, if nothing else, had remained the same about him.

"As my aunt has said, Miss Willows," he said, finally turning his attention toward Cassandra. "I would greatly like for you to design a gown for each of my sisters. They have long desired one of your creations, and I believe in indulging one's desires when one can."

Though his words were utterly proper, the expression in his eyes was heated. Cassandra swallowed hard. What was his game? Why bring her here, in front of his family, and toy with her? Why force her to tiptoe around the dangers of their being together in public?

Was this punishment?

No, she didn't see that in his stare. Heat, yes. An amused twinkle, perhaps. And something a bit deeper, a kindness she hadn't seen there before.

But no malice.

"Miss Willows?" he repeated, blinking as she stared at him in silence.

She shook her head to erase her thoughts and concentrate. "While I am flattered that you wish to have one of my designs," she began, giving the girls an apologetic look over her shoulder. "I must tell you how behind I am on my work." Now she gave Nathan a harder stare. "I have been *much interrupted* of late."

He seemed to be suppressing a grin, for the corners of his mouth twitched, which of course brought her attention fully to his lips and made her think of the last time he'd kissed her. He had tasted her like fine wine, using every inch of his lips and tongue and even his teeth to bring her ultimate pleasure.

Her thoughts must have shown on her face, for his smile faded and his eyes darkened with growing lust. He shifted somewhat uncomfortably and said, "Certainly you could fit an additional two gowns into your schedule, if you were properly compensated."

Cassandra drew back. It didn't seem like he was talking about money. "The compensation would have to be tempting, indeed."

"I promise you, it shall be. Perhaps you can measure my sisters and speak to them briefly about fabrics and colors and whatever else it is that you seamstresses go on about. Then you and I can speak about the price."

She tilted her head, exploring his face carefully. Under normal circumstances, she would never, *ever* measure first and negotiate later. But Nathan seemed to be asking her for something. Not demanding, not blackmailing . . . asking.

Sadly, he was impossible to deny.

She bobbed her head once. "Very well," she said softly, blocking out the girls' squeals. "My things are in my carriage."

"I shall have a servant fetch them," Lady Worthington said, exiting the room.

As the girls chattered excitedly behind them, Cassandra continued to look up at Nathan. "I am doing this because of my history with your aunt," she whispered.

He gave her a half smile, as if he didn't believe her. Nor should he, as it was a terrible lie.

"I understand."

"But I expect the compensation to be worth the trouble, my lord," she continued, never breaking their gaze.

His hand stirred at his side, fingers clenching. She stared at him in shock as she realized he had almost touched her with familiarity in front of his family. But instead, he forced his hand back down and shrugged one shoulder.

"I look forward to our negotiation with great anticipation," he all but purred, then stepped away as his aunt returned with a servant bearing Cassandra's work tools.

She shivered as she put her back to him and began to sort through her things. In truth, she was looking forward to their "negotiation" as well. Although there was nothing she could truly gain from spending more time with Nathan other than a broken heart.

Nathan had been well aware, even years before, that Cassandra had an interest in sewing. When he met her, she had already begun working in her father's shop, helping him with his tailoring business. She had sometimes spoken about her love of design and "the art of the needle," as she called it.

But he had never watched her in action. It hadn't even occurred to him to do so, for once he decided to marry her, he assumed she would never sew again, aside from some kind of ladylike needlepoint. So why bother?

Now he watched with wide-eyed interest and respect as she swiftly went about the business of measuring his youngest sister. She was efficient, each movement filled with economy as well as grace. And she had a remarkable eye, steering the girls away from colors that did not suit them without hurting their feelings and urging them toward the most flattering fabrics and designs.

And she did it all with a passion in her eyes that was only matched by her passion in his bed. For the first time, he realized she had far more than an interest in her work. She had a love for it. And she had become a great success by pursuing that love.

Nathan was shocked to find he was proud of her for that. Proud of how talented she was. And aroused as much by her talent as he normally was by her body. She brought so much passion to her work that he was beginning to think he ought to let her "measure" him as well.

Cassandra made a final mark in the small notebook she held in her hand and then helped Lydia step down from the elevated stool where she had been standing, arms outstretched.

"I believe I have all I need for now," Cassandra said with a brief smile for the two girls. "I shall bring your gowns here in three days, along with your aunt's, for the final fitting."

His aunt smiled. "I shall make the arrangements for a good time with you, my dear. And I'll be certain that my nieces are here to participate."

Cassandra nodded, as she swiftly packed her things back into a bag. "If that is all, I will leave you. I have much to do."

When she said the last, her eyes darted away. Nathan wrinkled his brow. He had been so focused on everything else about her, he hadn't noticed how tired Cassandra appeared. And not just physically. He frowned. "Let me escort you, Miss Willows," he said, coming forward and taking her case before she could argue.

His sisters and his aunt all drew in sharp breaths in unison. Nathan stifled a curse. A man of his stature didn't go around carrying the bags of a lesser person. He allowed servants to do it. Christ, he should hardly be aware of Cassandra at all.

And yet she was the focus of all his attention.

"I must negotiate the price of these gowns with Miss Willows," he explained swiftly. "We can do that as we walk."

"A quick negotiation to be sure," his aunt muttered.

He shrugged one shoulder. "I am quite persuasive," he chuckled.

Cassandra stiffened at his side, but she made no move to take her items back from him. "I am sure, my lord," she said. "But I have not come so far in business by bending to just anyone's will."

He motioned to the door. "Then I look forward to a spirited discussion." He turned back as Cassandra exited in front of him. "Aunt, I shall depart after my discussion with Miss Willows. Adelaide, Lydia, I assume Mama is coming to fetch you?"

The girls nodded and Adelaide said, "Yes. But we will not breathe a word of our fittings, just as we discussed."

He smiled. "Very good. I shall see you later. Good day, Aunt Bethany."

His aunt grunted a response that he barely heard as he quickened his pace to catch up with Cassandra at the front door. She hardly looked at him as he fell into stride beside her.

"So what can I offer you for your hard work?" he asked softly, keeping his tone low enough that the silent butler who showed them out did not hear.

She sent him a side-glance. "How about ceasing your blackmail?"

The frank request made Nathan stop midway to the two carriages that awaited them at the base of the circular drive. Somehow he had expected a much sweeter "negotiation." But here Cassandra was asking for something he wasn't sure he was going to be able to give.

She stopped at her carriage, which was in front of his since she had arrived before him. She waved away the footman who was moving to step down and gripped the door handle herself.

"This is madness, Nathan, we both know it," she whispered. "Have you not gotten enough revenge upon me? Have you not proven that you still control my lust, my desire?"

Nathan stared at her tired face. Defeat lined her cheeks, darkened her expression to an undeniable sadness. "Cassandra—" he began.

She held up her hand to silence him. "Please, Nathan. I can't do this anymore. I can't—" She broke off, staring at the ground for a moment. Her breathing was labored, clear evidence of her struggle. "I can't—"

Before she could finish, her face paled to a terrifying gray and her knees buckled. Nathan bit back a cry as he caught her before she hit the ground.

She looked up at him, eyes unfocused and voice weak as she whispered, "Don't let them see, Nathan. Please don't let anyone see."

He didn't hesitate, just gathered her into his arms and got into her carriage. He called out for them to be taken to her home and then closed the door behind them, locking himself into the vehicle with Cassandra as her head lolled back against his chest and her eyes fluttered shut in a dead faint.

Chapter Twelve

Cassandra was having the loveliest dream. She was in Nathan's arms, his hands gentle as he stroked her hair. When he spoke to her, his voice was filled not with anger or revenge, but with concern . . . love.

"Don't leave me, love," he whispered, his breath warm on her skin. "Don't leave me again."

She smiled as she looked up at him through hazy eyes. He was so beautiful, so strong and so everything she had ever wanted and more.

"I never left you, Nathan," she murmured. "You have to believe that I never left you."

Something jolted in her dream and Cassandra blinked. It wasn't a dream at all. She actually *was* lying in Nathan's arms, his hands lightly stroking through her hair. And they were in her carriage, of all places, which explained the rocking and jolting.

Reality infused her delicious haze and she sat up, pushing at Nathan's arms in an attempt to escape. He held tight.

"Don't thrash about so, Cass," he said, his lips thin. "Just rest."

"I'm fine," she argued, though she stopped struggling. It was too hard when she was so damned tired.

"Do you always faint in the street when you are 'fine'?" he asked, arching a brow.

Cassandra moaned and covered her face with one hand. "In the street?" she whispered, her voice muffled. "He'll love that."

Suddenly her 'bed' of Nathan's lap was far less comfortable. When she peeked through her fingers at him, she saw that he had stiffened and was looking down at her through narrowed and dark eyes.

"He? Who is *he*?"

She shook her head. It was too exhausting to come up with a believable lie, so she settled on the truth.

"Your father, actually. He has made it perfectly clear that he doesn't approve of our renewed . . ." She hesitated. "Er . . . *friendship*. I'm certain if he does have spies following me, he will accuse me of manipulating you by collapsing."

Nathan's frown deepened. "So, he's having you watched, too? Of course he is. He would want to see what is happening from both sides."

Cassandra bit back a humorless laugh. "This all feels so

familiar, doesn't it? He had us watched and followed all those years ago, as well. He would have done anything to keep us apart."

She hesitated. He *had* done anything, after all.

Nathan shrugged one shoulder, but she could see that he was more troubled by his father's interference than he let on. "The difference is that I have lived on my own long enough that I don't care what he thinks. Or says."

Now Cassandra did laugh, though she felt more sadness than humor. "Oh, Nathan, of course you do. No matter what, you care very deeply for your father, and worry about what he thinks of you. You always have."

Nathan opened his mouth to protest, but she cut him off by pressing her fingertips to his lips.

"It isn't a disparagement, darling, merely a fact." She let her fingers trail across his lips gently and suddenly the carriage felt warmer.

Nathan's hands clenched around her, his fingers massaging her side, her hip as he stared down at her with focused, heated intent. Cassandra licked her lips and he let out a low groan that seemed to reverberate in every inch of her body.

But before he could do anything to fulfill the promise that sparkled in his blue eyes, the carriage rolled to a stop outside her townhome and rocked as her servants stepped down.

Nathan gave her a half grin that melted her even more than his touch. "Home at last."

She nodded and began to extract herself from his arms. "I can manage on my own," she whispered. "You should go back to your aunt's before there is more talk than there likely already is."

Nathan held tight. "My sisters and aunt believe I was going to depart after I walked you to your carriage," he argued. "And my driver has followed us and is pulling into your drive as we speak. So I am going to take you upstairs and be sure that you are well before I leave you."

Cassandra would have argued, but before she could say anything, the coach door opened and Nathan swept her up and carried her from the vehicle with complete ease.

As he moved toward the open front door, she struggled.

"Nathan, put me down this instant!"

"I can't," he said as he swept past her butler and called out, "You there, bring Miss Willows some brandy and a cool compress. She fainted a few moments ago."

Her butler's eyes went wide and he immediately moved to follow Nathan's orders. Cassandra puffed out her breath in a huff.

"Wilkes, you come back here! Wilkes, listen to me!"

But the servant was already gone. She flicked her gaze to Nathan's face as he carried her up the long staircase to her chamber. "You have no right to come in here and order my servants about and carry me around like you own me."

"Very true," Nathan said, as he pushed her chamber door open with his shoulder and entered the room. "But I'm doing just that regardless."

As he set her on the bed, Cassandra looked up at him.

"Why?" she whispered, unable to keep the aching break out of her voice.

He shrugged one shoulder as he lay down beside her, facing her. "Because it terrified me when you collapsed," he admitted softly. "And I need to assure myself that you are well. Whole. Unharmed."

She swallowed hard, tears stinging behind her eyes. Damn him for saying something so sweet. It almost made her forget what he was, what he knew, what he felt. When he looked at her the way he stared now, all she could think about was the man who said he loved her all those years ago. That younger man was alive in Nathan's eyes now. Looking back at her as a pure temptation.

She found herself leaning toward him, straining to meet the lips that were coming in toward hers. But before they could kiss, the chamber door opened. Cassandra jolted and scooted away to face the door and the intruder.

It was Elinor who stood at the threshold, her eyes wide and cheeks pale. She held the cold compress and brandy that Nathan had ordered the butler to bring upstairs a few moments ago.

"What in the world is happening?" her friend asked, as she rushed into the room. "Wilkes said you fainted and was bringing these up. Of course I came straight away." Elinor pursed her lips as she looked at Nathan, still sprawled across the bed as if it was a perfectly natural place for him to be. "And what is *he* doing here?"

Cassandra flopped down on the pillows with a groan. By the concern in her friend's eyes, this conversation was not going to be brief. She cast a quick side-glance at Nathan to find he appeared as frustrated as she.

And why not? After all, they had been interrupted in the carriage and now here in her bed.

As if in answer to her look, Nathan pushed himself off the bed and moved toward Elinor with purpose in his stride. "Miss . . . Clifton is it?" he asked, his tone filled with lord-of-the-manor haughtiness.

Elinor's eyes narrowed. "Clifford, actually."

"Yes." Nathan smiled, thin and not particularly friendly. "It is true that Cassandra did faint today. And as you can see, she is quite tired, so perhaps you can save your tirades and questions until after she has had some time to rest. In the meantime, why don't we take this—"

He plucked the tumbler of brandy from her hand and turned to set it on the table beside Cassandra's bed.

"And this—"

Now he snatched the cool cloth away from her friend and gently handed it to her.

"And *you* can run along." He motioned Elinor toward the door with one hand.

Cassandra shut her eyes briefly. This wasn't going to go well.

As expected, Elinor placed her hands on her hips with an outraged gasp. "I beg your pardon Lord Blackheart—"

"Blackhearth, actually," Nathan said, but his voice was filled with humor.

Elinor rolled her eyes. "Yes. You have no right to tell me *or* my friend what to do. As I understand it, you surrendered that right long ago!"

Cassandra jolted straight up into a seated position and stared at the two. Damn her friend for saying such a thing! That was exactly why Cassandra had never whispered a word about her past with Nathan. She didn't want *anyone* using that as leverage either for or against her.

Nathan cast a quick and remarkably worried glance at her before he stepped forward and caught Elinor's arm. "Come Miss Clifford, let us continue this conversation outside so Cassandra may rest." As he hauled her friend out the door, he sent her a brief look. "I will be back, I promise you."

As the door slammed behind the two, Cassandra flopped back on the bed with a moan. Her doors were well insulated, so she couldn't hear the argument that was surely taking place in the hallway. About her. To protect her. From both sides.

She laid the cool washcloth over her eyes and sighed. The last thing she wanted was the two most important people in her life coming to fisticuffs over her well-being, but she was just too tired to intervene. So she shut her eyes and made the assumption that both would come out of their showdown alive.

"This is all your fault!" Elinor Clifford cried just as Nathan shut the door to Cassandra's room.

He spun on her. "Why don't you keep your mouth shut until we get out of Cass's earshot?"

"We're out of it now," the other woman snapped. "You couldn't hear a battle through that door, Cassandra made sure of it."

She arched a brow with a cruel tilt of her mouth and Nathan flinched. He knew full well what Elinor was implying. Cassandra had insulated the door so that no one would hear her with her lovers.

And damn if that didn't sting every fucking time he imagined it.

"Besides, don't try to pretend to me that you give a damn about her welfare after what you've done. The reason she collapsed is because of *you*."

Elinor paced the narrow hall restlessly, casting dark glances at him from time to time that did their job in shaming him.

"And just how do you figure that, Miss Clifford?" he drawled, folding his arms and leaning back on the wall beside the bedroom door.

She pointed her index finger at him. "Why do you think she's utterly exhausted? Because of *you*. This is already her busiest time, just as the Season begins and all the ladies are scrambling to fill out their wardrobes with the latest fashions to one-up each other! But then *you* come along. She's been up every night for the past month, either working her fingers to the bone or waiting for you. Sometimes both."

Nathan's cocky smile fell. He had intruded upon Cassandra's work more than once, that was true, but he hadn't fully realized just how busy she was. But then he thought of her tired face when his aunt requested that she make two additional gowns. For a moment, he had seen Cassandra's frustration. Now he fully understood it.

"Why does she not refuse to fill some of the orders?" he asked. "If she is tired, she should rest."

Elinor stared at him like he was a daft child for a long moment. "Because, you ox, she isn't like you! She doesn't have a fortune at her disposal that she can access to live a life of luxury. If she refuses the powerful women of your sphere, they will go to another seamstress and they might never return to Cassandra. If enough of them find a *modiste* they like better, she will be ruined. So she has no choice but to fulfill the orders and bow to your blackmail. Even if it kills her."

Nathan felt his nostrils flare. Elinor was being dramatic, of course, but perhaps not as much as he would like. When he thought of Cassandra's ashen face as she fell into his arms, when he recalled how unresponsive she had been to his initial attempts to rouse her . . . it terrified him.

"And don't forget this, my lord," the other woman continued. She moved toward him, all accusation and disgust. "If you are taking her to bed repeatedly, there is always the chance that she is breeding. Men of your stature hardly ever give a damn about that consequence, but one symptom of such a situation is fainting."

Nathan swallowed hard. Elinor was off the mark, of course. He had only lost control and filled Cassandra with his seed once in the time they had reunited. That was only a few days before and he knew enough to realize that her faint today was not a symptom of pregnancy.

But that didn't erase the fact that her friend's words were true. When he lost control inside of Cassandra, he had created a chance, however small, that she could carry his child.

Their child.

Years ago, he had yearned for that possibility to be a reality. He had sometimes watched her and tried to imagine what their children would look like. Would they inherit her auburn hair or his dark? Would they have her green eyes or the blue that streaked its way through his family?

When he and Cassandra parted, he had shoved those fantasies, those shadow children away, denying he had ever wanted them. Now they returned, dancing on the edge of his mind, taunting him with the future he had once craved. One he had lost in the midst of anger and betrayal.

He shook his head, hoping to clear those thoughts away, though he wasn't entirely successful. He met Elinor's heated stare with an even expression.

"Hear this, Miss Clifford," he growled, moving closer to accentuate his words. "You know nothing about my intentions when it comes to Cassandra. So why don't you simply do your best to assist her with her business and let us worry about what we are and aren't doing?"

Elinor opened her mouth for a sharp set down, but Nathan turned away before she could speak.

"I'm going back to Cassandra now. You are no longer needed today."

He opened the chamber door and shut it in her face, turning the key so that she could not intrude upon them again. When he moved into the room, he stopped.

Cassandra still lay on the bed, the cold cloth resting on her eyes. But even without seeing them, he could tell by her steady, deep breaths that she was asleep. He had a choice. He could leave. Or he could climb into the bed beside her and stay. Not for passion, not for sex, not for blackmail. Just because he wanted to be with her when she woke. To make sure she was fully recovered.

The latter was his only choice. Drawing a deep breath, he pushed his boots off one after the other, being careful so they didn't clatter against the wooden floor. Then he carefully took a place on the bed beside her. For a long time, he simply stroked her hair as she slumbered.

The quiet of the room was as good for him as it was for her. Because everything had just become far more complicated.

Chapter Thirteen

Cassandra lay in her bed, her eyes still closed. It was too luscious to lie under the warm sheets and heavy coverlet. Once she opened her eyes, she would be forced to get up and work and fight with Nathan and do a hundred other things she dreaded with all her heart.

For one, she would be forced to remember that she had fainted like a ninny. She groaned. Of all the people to collapse in front of, she had to do it in front of Nathan. Now he likely saw her as weak, he'd probably marked this down as another way to manipulate her.

Except that he had seemed truly concerned in the carriage. And he had told her how afraid he was here in her bed. The memory made her shiver and her eyes came open, only to find that she wasn't alone. Next to her, lying on his side just like she was, facing her, was Nathan. His eyes were shut and his breathing was deep and steady in sleep.

She stared. She couldn't help it. When he was awake, they were constantly at odds, battling for control and the upper hand. She didn't dare just moon away at him for fear he would take ground from her if she did. Now doing so was perfectly safe. *Nathan* was safe, unable to seduce and manipulate and push.

By God, he was beautiful. His black hair was so shiny and thick that she couldn't help but reach out and catch a strand between her fingers and rub its silkiness. Relaxed in sleep, his face seemed younger, kinder . . . far closer to the young man she had loved all those years ago.

Slowly, his eyes came open, revealing startling blue so bright that she sucked in a breath. His eyes had always been a draw for her, even from the first moment she met him.

"It's been so long since I woke up beside you," he murmured, his voice still heavy with sleep. "Too long."

She shivered. They had spent the night together only once all those years ago, hiding out in the hunting lodge on his father's estate. They made love all night, talked into the dawn, and then he had asked her to marry him.

It had been the best night of her life. Nothing, not even the glittering balls she had attended as a mistress or the fantastic theatre shows, could compare to the joy she had felt as Nathan dropped to his knees and begged her to be his forever. At that moment, she had believed they could overcome everything. Anything.

"That night was from another lifetime," she whispered, stroking his hair one last time before she let her hand drop away to the space on the bed between them. It was only a few inches, but suddenly it felt like a canyon.

He nodded. "Much has happened since then, in both our lives, the good and the bad. We've both changed." He tilted his head slightly. "And yet here we are, somehow still together, still drawn to each other with the same intensity that we were then."

"But not the same feeling," she said, her voice soft. This was dangerous territory they were entering now.

His lips pursed, but not in anger, as she expected. Instead, he seemed to be contemplating that statement, analyzing if it were true. What he could be analyzing, she couldn't say. After all, Nathan had made it more than clear that he felt nothing for her beyond a drive to make her pay. Being with her was simply a way to fulfill his angry vow to force her to feel what she had lost by throwing him away.

"No, the feeling is not the same," he agreed, and she hated how disappointment flooded her. "But that is to be expected. I couldn't feel the same way for you as I did before I went to India. So much has happened since then. I'm not the same man, as you point out regularly."

He hesitated and his face and voice took on a faraway quality. "But even if we hadn't parted on poor terms, the years still would have changed our feelings for each other."

She nodded. Yes, he was right about that. When he left without even trying to find out what had kept her from him, she had realized that it wasn't love he ever felt for her. A fondness, a desire . . . perhaps even a way to rebel against his overbearing family. But not love.

If nothing had kept her from him and they *had* married that night in Gretna Green instead of being parted, at some point she would have realized his lack of true emotion toward her one way or another. That would have broken her heart. Not to mention that eventually, Nathan himself would have realized he didn't truly love her. By that time, he would have been trapped in a marriage with a woman far beneath his station in life. He might have come to resent her.

In the end, it was better this way.

She sighed and moved to roll away. It was far past time to rise from the bed and return to normalcy after these few brief moments when she could pretend nothing had changed. But Nathan caught her wrist, pulling her closer rather than letting her move away from him.

"I imagine sometimes what it would have been like if you hadn't made your choices."

She squeezed her eyes shut. "Do you, Nathan?" she managed past tight lips. She would *not* reveal the truth, not just because he riled her with his false assumptions. "And what do you imagine?"

He cupped her cheek, his rough fingers gliding along her skin and into her hair. He inched her closer and moved toward her so that their bodies were pressed against each other. Chest to chest, pelvis to pelvis, leg to leg. There wasn't an inch to separate them.

"You as my wife," he murmured, his voice rough and seductive as his lips moved to skim along her throat. Cassandra
clenched her fingers into fists as pure pleasure followed in the
wake of his kiss.

"I imagine what it would be like to wake beside you like
this every day," he continued, his fingers massaging her scalp
while his other hand glided down her back to cup her even
closer. "To know that you are mine. I imagine what it would
have been like if *I* had been the one to introduce you to all
those pleasures you learned from your lovers."

She shivered as he rocked against her and she felt the hard,
thick length of his cock nudge her even through the layers of
her gown and chemise. Her body revolted against her reason,
opening instinctively, growing wet and exquisitely sensitive
in preparation for the invasion sure to come.

She fought the tide, though she knew it was in vain.

"But you weren't," she said, hoping to anger him enough
that he would storm out.

He continued nibbling at her throat, though she thought
he hesitated just a fraction. Then he shook his head, the be-
ginnings of rough stubble making her back arch.

"No, I wasn't. So I merely get the benefit of all that experience, don't I? Don't we?"

Then his mouth slid to hers and she lost all hope that she
could deny him. Not when his tongue slid past her lips gently,
softly exploring her with a slow cadence that told her he was
in no hurry to end this.

For the first time, there wasn't even a hint of anger in his touch, no erotic punishment. There was only pleasure, only desire.

He pulled back. "I thought long and hard about what I could have lost when you fell into my arms outside your carriage today. And then I thought of what I did lose when we parted ways all those years ago."

She swallowed. When their faces were so close together there was no way to hide from each other. She could see his desperation, his fear, and deeper . . . the fact that he still cared for her, despite everything.

Which meant that he could see all she sought to hide. Her desire. Her need for him. Her sense of loss. And her love. Because she had never stopped loving him. She had tried to do so, fought to do so, forced herself to pretend she had managed that impossible feat. But now, their bodies pressed so close that they were almost one, their breath mingling, with him whispering such sweetness in her ear, she couldn't deny her feelings any longer.

She still loved this man. And it brought her no pleasure, only pain. She buried her head in his shoulder, kissing his neck so he wouldn't see her heart. She couldn't bear that now.

"I want to be with you," she whispered against his skin. "I want to feel you hold me."

She didn't add that it would be for the last time. Because now that she had acknowledged her feelings for him, there was no way she could let this blackmail, her surrender go on. She would have to end this.

But she shoved those thoughts aside and instead crooked

her knee over his hip. He ground up, his erection finding her entrance through the layers of clothing. She sighed as he arched into her, rubbing her clit and sending tremors of pleasure through her.

He rolled, sliding her beneath him as he laced his fingers through hers. Holding her hands against the sheets, he dropped his mouth to hers and kissed her.

It was unlike any kiss they had ever shared before. Sweet and filled with longing, tasting of pleasure and deep desire. She drowned in his kiss, lifting herself into it, tangling her tongue with his.

When he drew back, his eyes were glazed, as surprised as she was. He pinned her with his stare.

"You are mine," he whispered.

She nodded. There was no denying that. She would never love another man like this. She would never touch another man like this, or be touched by him in this way.

In some way, she would be forever Nathan's. Even when he married another. Even when he forgot her.

He glided his hands down her sides, his palms cupping and lifting her breasts as he eased lower. He found the buttons along the front of her wrinkled gown and slowly unlooped each one from its hole. She arched into each moment, waiting breathlessly to be revealed to him, and to reveal him in return.

Her gown parted, the fine silk folding back to expose her sheer chemise beneath. Nathan muttered a curse at what he saw and she smiled. She always felt beautiful with him, like some goddess that he was driven to worship. Her lush body, which was not in fashion currently, was still something to be proud of when he looked at her with glazed eyes and shaking hands.

"I want to taste you," he moaned, his mouth coming down to her collarbone. "All of you."

She jolted at the suggestive words. A heated gush of moisture flowed through her, settling between her thighs, pulsing at her clit. She had no doubt he would make good on his promise that by the end of tonight she would be highly pleasured in every way.

And she could show him her love in the process. Even if she could never vocalize it. Her body would say what was in her heart.

He glided his mouth down her skin, pulling at her gown and her chemise to bare her more, but the fabric would only stretch so much. Finally, he gave a frustrated growl and sat up, pulling her along with him.

"Too many layers," he muttered, hardly coherent as he opened the remaining buttons on her gown and then pulled it down around her waist, followed by her chemise. She shivered as his hands brushed her skin as he worked. The side of his palm along her breast, the tips of his fingers brushing her stomach.

He didn't seem immune to those grazing touches either, for his voice was rough and strained when he said, "Lie back now."

Again she followed his instructions without argument or

comment. She liked him taking control. To be at his mercy as he urged her to lift her hips so that he could slide her dress and underthings away. Now she was naked aside from her stockings and her slippers. He caught his breath as he tossed her gown away off the side of the high bed.

"I could stare at you all day," he murmured, as he settled next to her and stared at her body from head to toe. "I could have someone paint a portrait and never tire of it."

He reached out and stroked the back of his hand against her collarbone. She stiffened, unable to stop herself from arching up into his hand. He chuckled softly and began to glide his hand back and forth, swish by swish, down the length of her body.

"But an artist could never capture your beauty in reality," he said, his fingers teasing over her distended nipples just for a moment before he continued his journey downward. "And I wouldn't want anyone else to see you posed like this."

She smiled despite herself, but her smile faded as he swept his hand over her lower belly. She tensed, ready for the pleasure of his touch at the juncture of her trembling thighs, but it never came. Instead, he scooted down the bed and wrapped his big, hot hands around her thigh.

"Nathan!" she gasped, jolting as he found a new sensitive spot that she hadn't realized existed.

He chuckled, wicked as he began to roll her stockings away, first on one leg and then the other.

"I believe you are the most responsive woman I have ever had in my bed," he growled. "You will sob with pleasure with just the lightest touch. I think you've even come before without stimulation."

She nodded, still shivering from his touch. She had almost come just then and he had only stroked her thigh in a new way. But she couldn't just let him be the wicked one tonight. She wanted to make *him* pant and beg and shiver like he did to her.

"Nathan, I have come a few times just from thinking about you. No touch necessary at all," she purred, raising herself up on her elbows and giving him her best come-hither look.

Her words clearly affected him, for his hands fumbled as he pulled her stockings over her knees. He looked up at her, blue eyes bright and focused as a bird of prey.

"Have you?" he whispered. "Show me."

She arched a brow. What she had said was true, but she wasn't totally certain she could reproduce the powerful, unexpected moment on cue.

"Finish what you started," she ordered with a teasing grin. "And I will."

His mouth quirked into a hint of a smile and he went to work unlacing her slippers. Then he tugged them off one by one, tossing them over his shoulder to clatter against the floor. Finally, he tugged each stocking free and let them flutter away.

She was naked, at his mercy.

"Your turn, Cass," he murmured, sliding away so that he no longer touched her. "I want to see you come merely by thinking about me. And explain how you do it."

Cassandra settled back against the pillows. "It was a fantasy," she explained, keeping her gaze firmly focused on him. "I was lying in bed, too exhausted even to pleasure myself."

He nodded, but she thought she saw a flash of guilt in his eyes.

"But I couldn't stop thinking of you," she whispered. "I had been to a party a few days before and I started imagining what it would have been like if you came to me there, in the middle of all those men and women of my class."

"And what did I do?" he said softly, but she heard the tension in his voice and saw it lining his face. He was already aroused just by the idea of what she was describing. It was taking every ounce of his control to keep himself from lunging across the bed and slipping his fingers inside of her to make her come.

She shivered, but didn't break her gaze from his.

"I imagined you would come into the room and cross the dance floor to find me. That you would want me so much that you wouldn't care who knew or saw. In my fantasy, I tried to tell you we should go somewhere private, but you were like a beast, possessed by need and desire."

Her breath was coming shorter now as she stared at Nathan, but continued to picture her fantasy in her mind. She could see it so clearly.

"In my mind, you grabbed me, kissing me like you were hungry for me. A starving man finally given sustenance."

"And in your fantasy, did you resist?" he asked, shifting on the bed.

She shook her head. "I tried, but what you wanted was so powerful, so overwhelming that I couldn't resist. Even as you tore my gown and bared my body to the room full of onlookers who were now gathered around us."

"Watching?" he whispered.

"*Leering*," she responded, holding his gaze steady. Her body was beginning to react to both his stare and her fantasy. She was wet and tingling, her pussy contracting around emptiness as it searched for fulfillment.

"And what happened next?"

She lifted her hips, never touching herself even though she ached to do so. "You thrust my legs apart, rubbing your fingers along me, pushing yourself inside until I was . . ." She caught her breath as pleasure began to make her twitch. "Until I was shivering and ready. And the crowd was moving closer, then. Watching, getting aroused just by seeing us together."

"They must have begun to respond to each other, too," he urged, sitting up straighter. "The men touching the women, the women moaning and jealous of your pleasure."

She jerked out a nod, his rich voice ratcheting up her desire and pleasure all the more.

"Finally you couldn't wait any longer. You mounted me, as randy as an animal. You filled me with your cock." Her breathing was so harsh now that she could hardly speak. "You fucked me right there, hard and fast, in front of a roomful of strangers. And I came."

The moment she said the final sentence, her body trembled

around the emptiness. She tipped back her head and the orgasm rushed through her like thunder, sweeping her away and making her body jolt and shiver.

She cried out, clinging to the bedclothes, well aware that Nathan was watching her and that knowledge only heightened her release.

But then suddenly he wasn't only watching. She felt the bed shift as he moved. Without preamble, he moved between her legs. She opened to him and cried out when she felt his tongue spear her channel, filling her with wetness before he stroked up to suckle hard on her clit.

Her orgasm increased in intensity and her cries turned to screams as he held her down with one hand and stroked her with the other, all the while alternating between filling her with his tongue and using it to stroke her clit.

She writhed beneath the pleasure, but it wasn't enough. She wanted more. She wanted to return the pleasure. To make him cry out as she did. To make him say her name.

"Let me please you," she cried out as she grasped his cheeks and pushed him away. Her body continued to pulse and she rolled her eyes back with a moan as she fought for focus.

"Together?" he asked, changing position to lie on his back beside her. He fumbled with his trousers, pulling and yanking until he could kick them down around his ankles, and his ready cock bounced free of its confines.

She nodded, unable to form coherent words when she was so lost in release and pleasure and desire. Instead she moved, positioning herself so that she could take his hard erection between her lips, but straddled over his chest so he could continue his mouth's torments against her aching entrance.

Immediately, he went back to work with that wicked tongue and her orgasm continued as if he had never stopped. She cried out, stroking his cock in time to her own thrusts. Tears streamed down her cheeks, her body felt weak.

All she could do was try to make him feel the same way. With another husky cry, she took him deep into her throat, stroking her tongue over his velvety skin. He groaned against her flesh, but didn't slow the pace of his mouth or his fingers. She met him stroke for stroke, speeding up when he did, slowing down to torture when he tried the same tactic.

Soon she was utterly spent and he was panting beneath her, lifting his hips to meet her mouth, driving himself deep into her throat as he growled out terms of ownership and desire. She felt him moving to the brink, his cock swelling with impending release. She welcomed it, needed it.

But before she could claim her prize, he shifted, dragging her up his body and flattening her on her back before he covered her. He kissed her and she tasted her own release on his mouth, earthy and heady and utterly arousing. She drowned in the flavor and the knowledge that he had done that to her. Made her shiver and quake and beg.

She tore at his remaining clothing without breaking the contact of their lips. He helped her, shedding first his shirt, then the trousers that still clung around his ankles. She opened her legs, wrapped her thighs around the muscular curve of his hips, and lifted in invitation.

He took it immediately. His cock slid past her opening, sliding into her channel with no resistance. As he fitted himself completely into her body, they let out a simultaneous sigh of pleasure and lay still. He kissed her on and on, dragging her tongue into his mouth, thrusting in mimicry of what he would do with his hips in a moment.

But then he pulled back and looked down at her. The room had grown dimmer as they slept, but enough light remained from the fire that she could see his expression through the shadows. He was purely focused on her, watching her with such tenderness that her eyes stung with tears.

Nathan shuddered as Cassandra reached for his cheek, cupping it as they lay joined together. He covered her soft fingers with his own and they tangled, holding hands as he began to move in rolling, wavelike thrusts that filled and retreated. She clung to his hand, her eyelids fluttering.

"Don't leave now, angel," he murmured, desperate not to lose the powerful connection they now shared. If she closed her eyes, it wouldn't be the same. "Look at me. Let me see you."

She let out a cry, but kept her eyes open, gaze locked with his as the first wave of ultimate pleasure struck her. Their fingers squeezed together as she moaned and arched, slamming her hips into his from below. Her inner muscles worked him, milking and releasing his cock in perfect time to his thrusts. But it was the look of pure pleasure on her face and the way she never looked away that really drove him over the edge.

His seed began to move and he let out a low, guttural

cry before he withdrew from her clenching body and spent himself. His heart throbbed as the last tremors of pleasure rocked him.

Nathan rolled to his back, dragging Cassandra with him as she settled her head into his shoulder with a contented, shivering sigh. He looked down at her with a smile.

"That was amazing," he said softly.

She nodded, her stare holding his evenly. "It was." She sat up a little, resting her chin on her hands against his chest. "Nathan, I want you to know that no matter who I was with, no matter what I did or learned . . . there was never anyone like you. There never could be."

He drew back, surprised that she would admit such a thing to him. Surprised but also proud. He knew the kind of men Cassandra had been with; he had met them and heard of their reputations. Surely, she had felt pleasure from their bodies.

"No matter what happens," she continued, her fingers smoothing his skin in little circles, "you will always remain with me."

His smile faded. No matter what happened. Of course, she was referring to their eventual parting, the inevitable moment when he let her go . . . on his terms . . . and went about the serious business of finding a wife. That was what he had planned, wasn't it?

He glanced at the little clock beside her bed and stifled a curse. "I must go now."

She nodded, no hesitation in her eyes. She made no effort

to stop him. That should have made him happy, but somehow he wished she cared enough to hold him. To ask him to stay with her all night.

But he couldn't, even if she requested it. He was due at another endless party, and this one his mother and father would attend. Since he had no doubt that his father was having him followed, the old man would know if he stayed all night with Cassandra. And Nathan wasn't up to yet more lectures on his future.

Especially since he already couldn't have the one future he had once longed for.

He pushed out of the bed and grabbed for his abandoned clothing. As he put himself back together, he watched Cassandra from the corner of his eye. She was staring, quite blatantly, as he dressed. And from the twinkle in her eyes, she was enjoying his accidental show.

Perhaps he could return in a day or two and give her the show in reverse. She would probably laugh if he stripped for her like a showgirl onstage. And then moan when he reminded her what he could do with his body.

He bent down and pressed a kiss to her lips, lingering for far too long as he enjoyed her taste, the memory of the passion they had just shared. Then he moved toward the door.

"I will return, Cassandra," he whispered.

She smiled, but there was something sad in her stare as he moved away. "Goodbye, Nathan."

With difficulty, he left the room.

★ ★ ★

Long after Nathan had gone, Cassandra lay in the growing dark of her bedchamber, staring up at the canopy above. He was everywhere around her now, his scent clinging to the sheets and her skin, her memory placing him in her chair, in her bed. He would taint this place forever. Just as she had feared the first time he entered, she could never look at the room the same way again.

Because soon enough he wouldn't ever be in this room again.

Years ago she had been naïve. Filled with girlish love for Nathan. She had foolishly believed that they could overcome his elevated status. That they could overcome the disapproval of his parents and Society.

More than that, she had believed his feelings were as powerful as her own and that they were all that mattered.

Time and heartache had changed all that. She knew now that there was no way the daughter of a tailor, a woman who made gowns for the rich, a woman who made toys for their husbands and lovers . . . she could never be accepted by Society.

If they were together, they would be shunned, locked out of the sphere he had grown up in, reveled in. So they could not marry, even if he wanted to marry her again. Which he didn't. It was clear that the best she could get would be an offer to be his mistress.

In some way, even that would be all right if they truly loved each other. She could live with being second choice, with seeing him raise sons and daughters with some prissy daughter of a titled lord, if she only knew she owned his heart.

But she didn't. She had recognized that the moment he was told she had betrayed him . . . and believed it without hesitation. He still *did* believe it, even as he came to her and held her and made love to her again and again and again. Some part of him still despised her for "her actions" on a long ago night.

No, Nathan didn't love her. He cared for her, she had seen it today. He lusted for her still, probably in spite of his own intentions and angers.

But that wasn't enough.

He had promised to return to her in a day or two. That gave her ample time to prepare herself. Practice her speeches. Be ready for the worst.

Because the next time she saw him, she would have to do the impossible.

She would have to let him go, once and for all.

Chapter Fourteen

*N*athan spun around the room, his hands positioned along the curve of a woman's hip as he turned them deftly in the country dance. She looked up at him, brown eyes wide and fawn-like, her smile coquettishly inviting. And he realized he had no idea of the woman's name, even though they had been dancing and talking for a few moments.

"So tell me about the fashions in India, my lord," the young lady said with a smile. "Or could you even call what those savages wear 'fashion'?"

Nathan pursed his lips at his companion's harshly chosen, ignorant words. But a vicious set down wasn't really appropriate in their current setting, so instead he forced his own tight smile.

"Actually, the women there wear what they call a 'sari,' a

long swath of brightly colored fabric that they wrap around themselves."

He smiled as he pictured Cassandra in such garb. How beautiful she would be among those women. And how excited she would be, as a seamstress, to learn new techniques and discover new colors and fabrics. He was certain she would adore India as much as he had grown to love it.

"It sounds positively scandalous!" his partner squealed, her sharp tone dragging him away from his pleasant daydream. "Their women must all look like they are . . . are . . . common *street* women."

She blushed as she said it and Nathan realized she was naively referring to whores.

He blinked a few times as he stared at the young lady. God, she was empty. A pretty vessel, but insubstantial and with no real purpose. She had spent her whole life being sheltered and prepared for a future existence exactly like her past one. She would ultimately become mistress over a family identical in every way to the one she had been raised in.

She had no humor, no free thought, no dreams or goals, at least that he could see from their albeit brief discussion. And she was the best of a bad lot that he had met over the past few weeks. Not one of those women sparked his interest. Not one of them made him feel even a twinge of the draw he still felt toward Cassandra, who was forever surprising and impressing him with her mind, her body, and her soul.

"You are looking at me in a very strange way," the young woman in his arms cooed as the music came to an end. "Perhaps you would like to take a walk in the gardens with me?"

Nathan blinked a few times. "No!"

She stepped back, yanking her hands from his as her cheeks filled with dark color. "No?" she repeated.

He shook his head and tempered his tone. "I only mean that your chaperone is approaching, and I have already promised the next dance to a very insistent young lady who would likely follow us if we were to go into the garden together."

That seemed to appease his partner, for her high color left her cheeks and she smiled. "Perhaps another time, then."

Then her chaperone arrived, talking boisterously about good matches and uniting families. Nathan stood for it for a few laborious moments before he slipped away and headed straight for a drink.

He stared around the room as he took a sip of watered down sherry. How different was he from all these people? He had grown up in the same circumstances, with the same rules and regulations and goals pounded into this head by his father. He had been just as empty as he had secretly accused his dance partner of being.

Until he met Cassandra. Only then had he felt alive. Free. Full, and in the best sense, for she had opened his eyes to a whole new set of feelings and interests. She had made him dream of love, regardless of its effect on his standing. When he was with her, he had forgotten standing altogether.

He still did. Even in his anger, when he had made snide comments about finding an "acceptable" bride, that hadn't been what was in his heart. The distance he maintained between them was about her lies and betrayal, never about her status.

Those things hadn't been resolved, and yet he still had feelings for Cassandra. Deeper and more powerful than the ones he felt all those years ago. He wanted her. But more than that, he found himself still *liking* her. Her quick-wittedness, her humor . . . those things drew him in as much as her lush and willing body.

"You must be the famous Lord Blackhearth."

Nathan shook out of his reverie and turned to find Stephan Undercliffe standing beside him. He jolted at the sudden appearance of Cassandra's former lover.

"Mr. Undercliffe," he drawled when he had regained his composure.

"You know, there is far better liquor in old Whipplesham's parlor. Care to join me for a spot?" the other man said, motioning to Nathan's drink.

Nathan stared at the unsatisfying spirit swirling in his glass, then back to his companion. Although he despised the sight of Undercliffe since he knew the bastard had been in Cassandra's bed, at the same time he might learn something of use from him.

And he did badly want a strong drink.

"Very well, sir. Lead the way," he said, motioning for the door.

They walked through the winding halls of the Whipplesham home in silence, though it was anything but companionable, until they reached the parlor. There was a tension that hung between them, an unspoken animosity that clung to the air and charged every movement. Nathan knew why he hated Undercliffe, but judging from the stiffness in the other man's shoulders, the feeling was mutual, though he had done nothing to the other man that he could recall. And he intended to find out why.

As he shut the door behind them, Nathan said, "It is interesting that both of us know of each other, although we have never been properly introduced."

Undercliffe crossed to the poorboy across the room and made two drinks. When he turned back and held out a glass to Nathan, he was smiling that wicked, knowing smile that Nathan had hated when he saw it at the Rothschild gathering.

"Well, I could very well know you because you are the prodigal son returned, the man whose name is on everyone's lips." He tilted his head. "How could you know me?"

Nathan took the offered drink and downed a swig before he said, "I *could* know you because you were pointed out to me at the Rothschild gathering a week or so ago."

Undercliffe laughed. "Yes, you glared holes into my new waistcoat. I shall have the bill sent to you."

Nathan's mouth twitched with a strange urge to laugh, but he didn't allow it. "But those aren't the reasons we know each other, Mr. Undercliffe, are they?"

Undercliffe set his drink down. His focused gaze had gone from humor-filled to hard. "No. Indeed they are not. I believe the true reason is that we share a mutual acquaintance. Cassandra Willows."

Nathan arched a brow, surprised that this man would so blatantly bring up Cassandra. But then again, he had to respect Undercliffe's brutal honesty.

"Yes," he acknowledged, filled with caution. "That is true. I am aware that you know her."

"I more than know her. She is one of my best and closest friends," Undercliffe said as he took a seat in the closest plush chair and dug into his vest pocket for a cigar. He chewed on it without lighting it as he stared up at Nathan. "Did you know that someone is blackmailing her?"

Nathan fought not to flinch. "She told you that?"

"Yes, a few weeks ago. Some cad, some bastard, who is threatening to ruin her."

"Hmmm," Nathan murmured, noncommittal since he felt he owned this man no explanation.

"Actually, I thought the culprit might be you, sir." The other man arched a brow. "I mean, you two do seem to share . . . *something*."

"You've been spying on your so-called friend?" Nathan asked, fighting to remain as calm as Undercliffe seemed to be. He wasn't about to give up even a quarter to the man.

The other man didn't smile. "If she is being threatened, damn straight I'll do anything to uncover more information. And the only new man in her life is you."

Nathan watched Undercliffe for a long moment before he acknowledged the truth with a negligent shrug of one shoulder, nothing more.

Undercliffe's nostrils flared ever so slightly. "I see. Then tell me, my lord, do you intend to make good on your threats and ruin her? Because know this, if you do, I have the capability of making your life quite uncomfortable. I may not have the clout or the standing that you do, but I do have my own means. And I think you know that Cassandra has *other*, far more powerful friends."

Nathan arched a brow, truly surprised. "You are threatening me?"

"Only if you are threatening her." Undercliffe did smile now, though there was nothing friendly about it. "I'm sure you know Cassandra and I once shared . . . *something*, as well. I cared a great deal for her, I still do. So you had best watch yourself with her."

Nathan stepped closer, but Undercliffe stayed in his chair, just looking up at him with a bored expression. Nathan clenched his fists at his sides.

"You don't know a God damned thing about me, Mr. Undercliffe," he said, his voice low and even. "Or Cassandra, for that matter. And I would thank you to stay out of my arrangement with her."

The other man raised his glass in mock salute, but didn't reply. And he didn't make any move to stop Nathan when he turned on his heel and stalked from the room, filled with jealousy, frustration . . . and guilt that he could no longer deny.

When Cassandra had been informed that she had a gentleman caller, she assumed it was Nathan, returning to her at last after a two-day absence when she had alternated between working until her eyes blurred and crying, since she had to let him go. She trudged to the parlor, her feet leaden. This was it. She had no choice but to send him away and hope . . . pray . . . that he could accept it.

She opened the door and drew in a breath to steel herself, but the man who rose from her settee and turned to face the door wasn't Nathan. It was Stephan Undercliffe, and he held out a bouquet of her favorite roses as he gave her that crooked smile that had always made her laugh.

Today her eyes stung in response. Relief and disappointment merged as she closed the door behind him.

"Stephan," she managed to choke out as she reached for the bouquet.

His smile faltered a bit, but his voice remained light as he responded, "Beautiful roses for my beautiful Cass."

She took the flowers. Already, an industrious servant had deposited a vase filled with water on the table across the room. She took the opportunity to busy herself by arranging his gift in the waiting receptacle.

"You should not have brought these, Stephan, though they are lovely."

She heard him move toward her a few steps, though he never went so far as to force his touch upon her. Stephan had always been gentle, coaxing rather than demanding, as if he had sensed she was broken by her past, even though he never pried. Today was no different.

"I needed to see you," he said softly. "And I knew they were your favorites. Though I've never seen you accept roses with such stark pain in your eyes, my dear."

Her fingers faltered in her work, but Cassandra forced herself to continue as if his keen observation didn't trouble her. She didn't want to be so easily read.

"Pain? No. I am tired, that is all," she said with a hollow laugh.

Now he did move closer and she felt his warm hands gently caress her upper arms. He turned her to face him, cupping her chin with one big palm and forcing her to look up into his eyes.

"You *are* tired," he agreed. "But the pain is about something emotional, not physical."

Cassandra felt tears sting at her eyes as she stared up at him, his expression so kind and accepting. He had always known her so well. In another life, she might have loved him. But she didn't. All her heart belonged to someone who would never look at her like Stephan did.

"I cannot talk about this," she stammered, moving away.

He let her go with a low sigh and for a long time the room was silent.

"I saw Nathan Manning . . . the great Earl of Blackhearth," he finally said, his voice filled with disdain as he spoke Nathan's name and exalted title. "I know he is the one who has been blackmailing you."

She caught her breath as she lifted her fingers up to cover her lips. "How do you know that?"

He tilted his head. "Even if your stricken expression hadn't given it all away, he admitted it when I confronted him at the Whipplesham soiree."

For a long moment, Cassandra was quiet, uncertain as to how to respond to Stephan. Even less certain of how she felt about the truth being exposed to her friend. She had been willing to tell him certain details, but she hadn't wanted anyone to ever know her association with Nathan. For too many reasons to count, making that fact public could only cause her trouble and heartache.

"I see," she finally whispered. "He bragged about it, did he?"

Stephan's brow wrinkled as if he were considering that question. Then he shook his head.

"I would love to tell you that he did, to tell you what a bastard he was about the whole disgusting business."

Cassandra clenched her fingers into fists as her stomach turned.

"But that would be a lie," Stephan continued softly. "In fact, he looked a good deal sicker about it than I would have expected. He seemed to take no pleasure in his actions."

Relief staggered Cassandra and she swayed a touch on her feet before she steadied herself. Even if she did intend to end it all with Nathan, she hated the idea that he was crowing over his blackmail. She didn't want to believe that of him. Not anymore.

"Of course, he didn't seem all that affected by my threats, either," her friend continued with a shrug of one broad shoulder.

Cassandra raced forward, grasping both of Stephan's hands in hers. "You *threatened* him?"

He hesitated, staring at their clasped fingers for a moment before he continued, his voice slightly unsteady. "Of course. Cassandra, you must know that I would do anything for you. Anything."

She drew in a sharp breath as she stared up at Stephan. There, sparkling in his eyes . . . was *love*. And not the kind she felt toward him, of friendship, of gratitude. It was romantic love. The kind she felt toward Nathan.

She moved to snatch her hands away, but he clung to them.

"Don't, Cass, don't," he pleaded. "I must tell you this, you must hear it."

She shook her head, knowing full well what he was about to confess, even before he said the words. "Don't say it, Stephan. Please don't say it. Your friendship means too much to me. Once you say it, it can't be taken back. And I don't feel that way for you. I wish to God I did, but I don't."

"Because you love him," he said, his voice dull and flat.

Cassandra swallowed hard. She knew the "him" Stephan referred to as plainly as he did. Her friend wouldn't believe her if she lied. He knew her too well.

Finally, she nodded. The tears she had been fighting for so long trickled down her face.

Stephan never removed his stare from her, just held her gaze with a sadness and disappointment that broke her heart. Then he lifted her hands to his lips and pressed a kiss on each one.

"I may not speak my heart, but I will still feel it. And if you ever change your mind, I will be here. Whether as your friend or . . ." He released her hands and gave a wave in the air that spoke volumes.

Cassandra stepped back. "I appreciate that, Stephan."

"And now we must decide what you will do about your Nathan Manning," he said, the light back in his voice, the seriousness gone like he had never almost vowed his love for her. "Because you clearly need help and I am the best one to give it. After all, I know you so well."

Cassandra swiped at her tears and laughed despite herself. "I suppose you do. And I admit that it would be a great help to talk about this with someone. I have been alone in it almost since the beginning. Elinor doesn't understand and I certainly can't discuss it with Nathan."

"No." Stephan poured himself a cup of tea with a dry laugh. "Most certainly not. Why face this with honesty and direct-ness? It is so much more fun to dance around the truth, dodge the reality of the situation, which is that you are in love with this man, you share some kind of unhappy past with him . . . and that he has feelings for you, as well. Why would you ever wish to deal with that head on?"

Cassandra flinched. Stephan was mocking her, and when he laid her problems out like he just had, it did seem silly. But the problem was that Stephan was missing one very large piece of the puzzle. The one thing she had never told any other soul. Not Elinor, not Nathan, not her parents.

Stephan didn't know what had happened to her the night she was to meet Nathan. The night he believed she had betrayed him.

"There is more to this than you know," she whispered.

He tilted his head. "Do you wish to tell me?"

She hesitated before she shook her head. She couldn't tell this man the secret she wouldn't confess to the man she loved. It wasn't fair to anyone involved.

"No."

He shrugged. "Fair enough. So tell me, what do you want from Nathan Manning? What do you *need*?"

Cassandra sighed. That was the heart of the matter, wasn't it? And asked directly, she could answer.

"I want him to let me go." Her voice broke shamefully and she cleared her throat. "I need to break from him, once and for all."

"You are certain?" Stephan seemed surprised. "Even though you care for each other?"

She laughed, humorless and pained. "If things were so simple, everyone would be happy. You know there are often complications that trump caring and respect and even desire to be together."

Stephan's lips pinched in pain before he nodded. "So you wish to end things before it gets harder."

She sighed. That was the perfect summation. "I do. But I don't know how to do it."

Her friend took a seat, steepling his fingers as he considered her troubles. Cassandra found herself holding her breath, awaiting some magical answer that Stephan would surely give.

"I think I know a way," he finally said, reaching for her hand. "It will involve deception. And it will likely end your affiliation with Lord Blackhearth permanently, so you must be certain that is what you desire."

Cassandra shivered before she took a seat across from him and leaned in closer. "I am certain. Tell me your plan."

Chapter Fifteen

*A*s the door to his office swung open, Nathan looked up from the paperwork spread out on his desk before him. He had asked not to be disturbed under the guise of doing work on one of his estates, but in reality, he hadn't been concentrating on paperwork about the best crops to plant or on a ledger that outlined how his people were paid. Instead, his thoughts had been consumed by Cassandra and plans about how he could continue to see her, be with her, even as he fulfilled his need to find a proper wife.

His butler gave him an apologetic nod. "You have a visitor, my lord. I tried to tell her you were not receiving, but she has anchored herself in the south parlor and refuses to leave until you speak to her."

Nathan's heart leaped. Only one woman would be so bold. He pushed to his feet. "She would not give her name?"

The servant shook his head. "She said you would guess."

"Indeed. Thank you, I shall handle this. Please do not allow us to be disturbed."

The butler bowed out with a murmured yes, leaving Nathan to stare up at his reflection in the large mirror that hung above his desk. The last time Cassandra barged into his home it had been for that sinful night of sex that hardened his body every time he recalled it.

But today she came to his parlor in the light of the afternoon. She didn't sneak in or bribe her way inside his chamber. She walked through the front door where any of his father's spies could see her.

If she was willing to allow her visit to be public knowledge, she must have something important to say.

He left the room and hurried down the hallway to the parlor. Outside the door, he paused and drew a few long breaths. Calm was key. Until he knew her intentions, he couldn't reveal his thrill at seeing her. Perhaps by the time this night was done, they would come to an agreement regarding a continued affair. One born of mutual desire, not blackmail.

Pushing the door open, he stepped inside. Cassandra was not seated, but paced around the room, hands clenched before her. When he closed the door behind him, she jumped and faced him. He couldn't help but notice that her expression wasn't one of desire, or need, or excitement. In fact, she looked like she was about to face a firing squad.

He made his own face unreadable in response.

"Good afternoon," he managed to say as he moved closer. "I did not expect you."

"I realize that, and I am sorry that I did not send word of my arrival first." When he advanced a second time, she stepped back. "I was afraid you would not see me and it was imperative that I speak to you today."

He motioned to the settee, but she shook her head. "I do not intend to stay long."

He frowned. This did not bode well.

He took the seat she would not and looked up at her with a disinterest he didn't feel. But he wasn't about to let her know that he wanted to yank her into his lap and kiss her until she was senseless. Until she forgot whatever upsetting thing that had to be said this very moment.

"You are very serious," he said softly.

She nodded, the movement jerky.

He shrugged. "Then say what it is you have come to say since you cannot escape me fast enough."

She stopped wringing her hands and looked down at him, her eyes filled with sadness. "I realize I am being short, but that is not my intention. You must understand this is difficult for me."

He nodded, unable to keep from softening in the face of her true upset. Whatever else was about to happen, he believed her statement to be true. This conversation was no pleasure for Cassandra.

"Speak, Cass," he said softly.

She squeezed her eyes shut briefly, then met his gaze with an even, strong expression. "You came to me a few weeks ago, making demands, using blackmail to get something you wanted. I allowed it, for I felt I had no choice. But . . ."

She hesitated and Nathan's blood began to roar in his ears as he waited for the remainder of the sentence. "But?"

"This is over, Nathan."

He couldn't help but buck to his feet in surprise. Although he had expected this conversation to be unpleasant when he saw Cassandra's expression, this was not what he had anticipated.

"Over?" he repeated, hating how his voice broke and revealed too much emotion, too much pain—even more than he had believed he felt. The feelings washed over him, burning like boiling oil, refusing to be ignored. But behind the pain, behind the confusion, something throbbed all the stronger. Love.

He blinked as he stared at Cassandra through the blur. He loved her. He had always loved her, even as he hated her. Even as he blackmailed her. He loved her.

And she was walking away from him again.

Her breaths came short and labored as she continued, "I have given you what you desired, and you have humiliated and controlled me enough to avenge whatever you felt I did to you in the past."

He arched a brow, his anger building. "Have I? You think a few weeks of minor discomfort mixed with ultimate pleasure can truly make up for the destruction of my life? The betrayal of the feelings I had for you all those years ago?"

She folded her arms, unmoved except for a slight twitch around her lips. "You may not think so, but *I* do."

He sneered at her, his anger bubbling and boiling to the surface. Anger was safe, it was strong. "Don't forget what I can do to you, Cassandra."

He hated himself the moment he said it, for the threat was an empty one now. Now that he recognized the twisted truth that he still loved this woman, despite all she had put him through, he realized it had always been an empty threat. He never could have destroyed her when it came down to it. But from the way Cassandra flinched ever so slightly, she believed he was threatening her rather than merely playing a desperate card to make her stay.

She lifted one shoulder delicately. "If you feel you must reveal my secondary life, expose me and destroy me . . . then so be it."

He drew back in pure shock. She was willing to be exposed?

She seemed to read his thoughts, for she sighed. "I have never been ashamed of what I do, of who I am . . . I won't let you make me ashamed. If you reveal me, then what will be will be."

"You'll be ruined," he reminded her.

A nod was her instant reply. "And perhaps *then* you will feel your own humiliation is avenged and you will be able to move on with your life. Either way, I will no longer be your plaything. This is a sick game, Nathan. You have a life to lead, as do I. Those lives never should have intersected in the first place, but now is the time to end it. Once and for all."

He moved forward a jerking step. "And what brought on this sudden epiphany that you don't give a damn what I do? What made you decide it was time to 'move on' with your life, as you put it?"

She sucked in a breath, but she held her ground as he crowded into her. Looking up, she met his stare.

"There is someone else, Nathan."

He stared at her. "What?"

She hesitated for a moment before she whispered, "I have renewed my relationship with my former protector, Stephan Undercliffe."

Nathan physically jerked away, spinning so he wouldn't have to look at her. He couldn't believe this was happening again. That she was revisiting the same betrayal that had torn them apart the first time. Especially since they had forged such a powerful bond during the past few weeks of passion, anger, and desire. He had felt that.

And she had too.

He stared with unseeing eyes at the opposite wall as every touch, every kiss, and every conversation they had shared flashed through his mind. When he turned back, she was still looking at him, unflinching.

Her words were correct, perfectly chosen to cut him to the bone. Her manner was exactly right, as well. She was stoic, her delivery of this mortal wound very matter-of-fact. It was all exactly right to make his rage overtake him, to make him turn away from her forever and never look back.

In fact, it was almost too perfect. Rehearsed, even.

And in that moment, he stopped believing her. She wanted him to think that she had turned to another. But in his heart, he knew it wasn't true.

He smiled a brittle smile. Anger boiled up in his chest. How dare she lie, using their painful past against him? That actually bothered him more than her "confession" that she had turned to another man.

"Forgive my language, my dear, but *bullshit*."

Cassandra flinched as Nathan spat the curse at her. How could he not believe her? He had been absolutely willing to believe the same lie all those years before. In fact, he *still* thought she had thrown him aside when she hadn't come to meet him that long-ago night.

She had been completely certain that he would accept as truth the same falsehood now, especially when it came from her own lips.

And yet he didn't.

"What I have told you is true," she croaked, but she didn't sound very honest, even to her own ears. "You can ask Stephan if you'd like. I'm sure he could be quite descriptive in his answers."

Nathan's nostrils flared, but he didn't turn away. *Why* didn't he turn away?

"I'm sure he would. That bastard would probably take great pleasure in making me seethe as I pictured the two of you tangled together in his bed."

Cassandra tensed as Nathan's face twisted with anger as he

said the last few words. But still, he didn't recoil from her. If anything, he moved closer, his big body almost touching hers. She shivered at the unexpected proximity. It was as much torment as his continued pressure for the true reasons she was turning away from him.

"But all his coarse descriptions won't make your lies any more true," he said when she didn't reply. "You are only using him in a futile attempt to make me walk away. But it won't work, my dear. You are lying, desperate to end things. And I want to know why."

Cassandra shook her head. This was enough. She wouldn't torture either one of them any further.

"I'm leaving," she whispered and moved toward the door.

His hand shot out and he caught her wrist, pulling her against him with just the slightest tug. "Not until you tell me the truth."

She pulled at her arm, but he held strong. Panic began to rise in her and she tamped it down. He couldn't see. He couldn't know. No matter how hard he pushed her.

"You are so sure of yourself," she panted, continuing to tug in the hopes that she could anger him enough to make him set her free. "So certain that I couldn't want another man after having you again. Don't allow your overconfidence to make you a fool, Nathan. I just don't want you anymore. Avoid this humiliation and release me."

Instead, he pulled her even closer. Her chest crashed against his, molding against him naturally, sucking in his heat. Against her will, she breathed in his scent. Even in the midst of anger and upset, she had to force herself not to sigh with pleasure.

"Your body betrays you, Cass," he said, his voice far softer now. "Even now you want me as much as I want you. You've told me more than once that you couldn't be forced to be with me if you didn't want this as much as I do. So why would you turn to another man? Even if you don't care for me, you are finding great pleasure in my bed."

He kept a tight hold on her imprisoned wrist, but with the other hand, he cupped her chin, tilting her face toward his. She blinked, fighting tears, fighting the need to lift her mouth to his. To declare that she still loved him as much as she had all those foolish years ago when she had been ready to throw away everything to be his bride.

"So unless you are in love with him, you shouldn't want to run," he continued.

She stopped tugging and forced herself to meet his eyes. She could end this if only she could declare she loved Stephan. If she could make Nathan believe that, he would let her go. He would never seek her out again.

"Are you in love with him?" he whispered, his mouth moving toward hers in a torturously slow descent.

She tried to nod, but found herself frozen. She opened her mouth, but the words just wouldn't come.

"Tell me," he pressed. "Do you love him?"

"Let me go," she finally whispered, and this time when she

pulled at her wrist, he allowed her the freedom. She immediately made for the door, but his legs were longer, his stride stronger, and he made it there before she could escape.

Flattening his palm against the wood, he held it shut, trapping her once again with the unyielding plane of his body.

"Why didn't you show up that night all those years ago, Cassandra?" he whispered.

Her gaze jerked up. He had never asked her that question. She had never been forced to escape his direct interrogation on what had happened that night.

"You know, don't you?" she asked, turning the question back on him as she prayed he would let the subject go.

He tilted his head and his stare was more intense than she had ever seen. She flushed under the focused scrutiny. He was forcing her to think about things better left unremembered. Making her fight against feelings and nightmares that had taken so long to overcome.

"I'm not sure," he said, and there was true confusion in his tone. "I thought I knew, but now . . ."

He hesitated and she shifted as she watched his mind work.

His voice grew softer. "Now, looking at you, seeing you use the past and realizing it is a lie . . . I wonder now if I did know the truth about why you left me standing in the rain, waiting for you to arrive and run away with me."

"Why question the past?" she asked, her shoulders beginning to shake even as she tried to stop it. "Why revisit something that only caused us both great pain?"

"Because I want to know," he growled. "I want to know why you didn't come. I want to hear it from your lips."

"No." She shook her head. The pressure was almost unbearable, the memories struggled to break free, and the pain was returning to stab at her. She had overcome this! She didn't want to go back. "*No.*"

He grasped her shoulders. "Tell me, Cassandra. If you want this to be done, if you want this to be over, then tell me the truth and then let us be done with it."

She shook her head. It wouldn't end with the truth. A new batch of questions and hurt would only just begin.

His lips pursed in utter frustration. "*Why* didn't you come to me? Why didn't you even care enough to show up and tell me face-to-face that you had changed your mind and desired another? Why did you throw away everything we had promised? Built? Dreamed?"

She lifted her chin. In all the years since that night, she had never been ashamed of what she had endured. She refused to be ashamed now.

"You want to know the truth?" she hissed, feeling the blood heat her cheeks. "You want to hear it so bloody much, Nathan?"

"Yes!" he shouted.

"I was attacked, Nathan. I was raped! Is that what you want to hear? Is that what you want to know?"

Chapter Sixteen

*N*athan released Cassandra's shoulders and staggered back away from her trembling form. His ears were ringing and his stomach clenched and roiled as he digested those words she had said. Those horrible, horrible words. The ones he instantly knew were true as surely as he knew his own name.

"Attacked?" His voice was hardly audible, even in the quiet room. He swallowed hard before he could continue. "Raped?"

She nodded, her eyes still turned away from his. Then she slowly faced him, meeting his gaze head on. Although pain at the memories he had forced her to relive lingered in her green eyes, there was no hint of shame sparkling there. Not one iota of self-blame.

Her strength awed him, silencing him for a full minute as he merely stared at her.

"Tell me," he finally whispered when he could force himself to speak.

He reached for her, but she moved away, refusing his comfort, refusing his touch. He flinched as he thought of how he had forced it on her, how he had held her against him more than once. The truth certainly explained her strong reaction when he held her captive the day after they made love. Why she struggled so much when he caught her wrist a moment ago.

He had made her think of horrible things, of a horrible man who had taken her body against her will.

She swallowed, her delicate throat working with the effort. "What is there to tell, Nathan?" Her voice started out hoarse but slowly gained in volume and strength. "I was on my way to meet you. It was late, it was dark. I was alone. A man stepped from the shadows alongside the road."

Nathan sucked in a breath and shut his eyes as he tried not to picture the horror of what she was describing. She said the words so plainly, a recitation that could just as easily be a list for her grocer. Until she paused and exhaled a breath like a sob. Only then did he feel how much the memories haunted her.

"At first I wasn't afraid. It was Herstale, after all, a place I had felt safe all my life. I asked if he was lost—" She stopped and her fingers clenched at her sides.

"You don't have to—" Nathan began, wanting to know,

but unable to force her to relive this pain when he saw her struggling.

She shook her head. "No. Now that I have started, you might as well know it all."

She drew a long breath and then continued, "He told me he was exactly where he needed to be. I saw his intent in his eyes and I tried to run, but he caught me. He was far stronger than I. I screamed, but no one was around to hear." She clenched her fists as she glanced downward. "I fought, but he took what he wanted. He held me until the next day, when he let me go."

"The next day?" Nathan repeated.

She lifted her gaze. "Yes."

She offered no other explanation, but he did not need it. It was plain what she had gone through in those long, horrible hours.

"Why didn't you find me? Tell me?" he whispered, longing to smooth her hair away from her face, to hold her, but her body language warned him away. Her stiff posture, her ramrod straight shoulders, they were a shield.

From him.

She shook her head. "I was bedridden for days afterward," she whispered. "By the time I was *able* to speak to anyone, you were long gone. Off to India to stew on your betrayal."

Nathan flinched. Jesus, what he had done to her.

"If I had known—" he began.

She cut him off with a sharp glance. "You *should* have known, Nathan. You should have known that I wouldn't merely abandon you without saying even a word of goodbye. You should have had that faith in me."

Her direct statement cut into Nathan's heart like a dagger. He had no words to give, nothing to explain or excuse himself. All he could do was stammer, "I-I am sorry, Cassandra."

But the words were empty and meaningless.

She shook her head. "You don't know how much I truly do appreciate that after all these years. But you needn't say it. There was nothing in that horrible night that I am thankful for, but there is something to be said for realizing that you did not truly love me. Love involves faith. Withholding judgment. You didn't do that. For some reason, you couldn't."

She turned away and moved toward the door. This time he didn't stop her, even though he wanted to so desperately. But he was frozen by her confession. By her words. Her accusations. Her cool statement that he hadn't loved her, or at least not enough.

Here he had spent the past few years believing the same thing of her.

She stopped at the entryway and her shoulders rolled forward in emotion and defeat. "We were never meant to be, Nathan. In the end, that would have been true whether I reached you that night or not. When I was *waylaid*, it only underscored that fact."

She glanced at him over her shoulder and her gaze was so filled with sadness and heartache that he could scarcely bear it. But he looked. He owed her that much. He owed her so much more.

"I'm leaving now," she whispered, turning the door handle. "I won't be back. And I ask you not to come to me anymore. We've both suffered enough, I think."

Then she slipped away, leaving Nathan alone in the empty room. Alone with his thoughts. With her words.

And he cast up his accounts into a waste bin.

Cassandra was in the carriage when she let the tears fall. She had been holding them back, choking on the pain, since Nathan began his relentless quest for the truth. Now they trickled down her cheeks as she lay on her side across the carriage seat and sobbed.

She had never told anyone the truth about her rape. Not even her parents or the doctor they had summoned when she arrived on their doorstep, battered and sobbing, once her captor released her. All she had said, over and over, was that Nathan hadn't been the one to harm her. After all, she had assumed the man she loved . . . the man who loved her, would arrive to find out what had happened to keep her from their meeting. She hadn't wanted her father to turn the dogs loose on him.

But he hadn't come.

Her parents had known she was hurt, known someone had done *something* to her. But they had been more concerned about helping her heal than uncovering the details. People of their stature and class had little luck at finding justice, so they often didn't bother to seek it.

After she had lain crying for a few long moments, Cassandra straightened up. Enough tears had been shed about that night. Ultimately, she had found the strength to overcome the horror. She had even become a mistress and forced herself to feel pleasure again. To remember that a man's touch could be good, could be beautiful.

She had overcome the past. No one could drag her back to that place. Not even Nathan.

In the end, the truth had set her free. If nothing else could stop him from pushing her, forcing her to his will, it was evident her confession had finally done that. He was so horrified, so stricken by the knowledge of the truth that she had faith he wouldn't pursue her again.

So it was over.

She smoothed her skirt as her carriage pulled to a stop in front of her pretty townhome. It was over. She had what she wanted.

Now she just had to forget about Nathan and move on with her life.

Nathan dug his heels into his horse's side, urging the animal to ride faster through the streets of London. After he was sick, he had fled the house, just wanting to run. Far away. And his horse was up to the task, darting around the traffic of the darkened streets, his hooves clopping on the cobblestones.

But the wind on his face, the smell of soot, the freedom of riding . . . none of those things could make Nathan forget why he was running.

Cassandra's confession had rocked him to his very core and

upended every belief that had driven him for the past four years.

Why hadn't he known that she had been attacked?

The events of that night ran through his head as he dodged an overturned apple cart and steered his horse through an alleyway.

He had gone to meet Cassandra, and he had waited all night in the pouring rain for her to arrive. When he returned home, his father had been waiting for him, sitting in the foyer with a letter in his hand. He had berated Nathan, calling him all manner of fool for throwing away his future for a common tailor's daughter.

At that point, Nathan had been ready to agree. It was hard not to when he was soaking wet and abandoned to the cold light of dawn. But perhaps, once he was dry and warm again, he might have considered the many reasons Cassandra would stay away from a meeting they had planned and anticipated for so long.

Except then his father had given him the letter. Something the Marquis had said was intercepted between Cassandra and another man. It had been in her hand, Nathan would have recognized it anywhere, for they had kept contact through love letters.

Even now, riding through London, *knowing* that the letter had been some kind of manipulation, Nathan still felt the anger—and the pain—just as keenly as he had all those years ago.

And he had believed it. When his father suggested time away from London, time away from England entirely, he had been more than happy to board the next vessel to India and lose himself in spices and drink and the foreign life he had led.

He jolted as he turned his horse one more time and found he had, without thinking, steered the animal to his father's townhome in London. Lights glittered from the large, clean windows. The family would likely be having supper, sharing wine and stories just as they had his entire life.

They would welcome him in, but he didn't want welcome and family comfort. He wanted the truth. The truth he had a sneaking suspicion only his father could provide.

A servant met him as he brought his horse up sharply before the marble steps that led to the front door. Nathan tossed him the reins without comment and stalked to the house. He pushed the front door open before the butler could reach it.

"Good evening, my lord," the servant stammered.

"Where is the family?" Nathan asked, but it was an empty question, for he was already making his way to the dining room where he could hear their voices and the clink of silverware and crystal.

"My lord, I can announce you, my lord—" the butler said, jogging to keep up with Nathan's long strides.

But Nathan had already slammed the door open, letting it hit the wall behind it with a satisfying, jarring smack.

The family turned at the loud noise and Nathan finally stopped his forward motion. His father sat at one end of the table, his mother at the other. His sisters sat together on one side and his place was empty on the opposite one, waiting for him to join the family tableau.

And it was somehow tempting to do so. To try to forget that everything in the past four years of his life had been built on a lie. A lie his father had perhaps been a part of.

But he couldn't forget. He needed the whole truth. Everything.

"Nathan," his mother said, getting to her feet and moving toward him. Her face was lined with concern the closer she got. "What is it? What is the meaning of barging in here with such dramatics?"

"Tell Adelaide and Lydia to go up to their rooms to finish their dinners," he replied, meeting his mother's eyes.

Was *she* involved in whatever trickery had been employed to make him lose faith in Cassandra? She had despised the idea of him marrying someone so common as much as his father had.

"Nathan?" she said softly, grasping his arm.

"Do it," he said, forcing himself to lower his voice.

She glanced down the table at his father. The Marquis hadn't gotten up, but his face had paled, almost like he wasn't surprised to see Nathan in this state. Nathan flinched at the guilty expression he had never seen his father possess. It was hard to look at when coupled with the gauntness illness had brought.

"Lydia, Adelaide," his father said, in a tone that brooked no refusal. "Do as your brother suggests."

He motioned to a servant to take the girls' plates.

"But—" Adelaide began, even as she pushed to her feet, her eyes wide and filled with fear and curiosity. Lydia rose beside her, clutching her elder sister's arm as she stared from her father to her brother.

Nathan shot Adelaide a glare that silenced her immediately and the two girls left the room with only quick glances over their shoulders. Once the servants in the room had followed and shut the door behind them, Nathan moved forward, his focus on his father.

"You gave me a letter," he said with no preamble.

His mother moved to sit beside his father and she looked at Nathan with confusion. "A letter? What letter are you talking about?"

"He knows." Nathan speared his father with a stare and his father did not look away. "He knows what I am referring to. That night, four years ago, you gave me a letter that your spies had supposedly intercepted from Cassandra."

His mother flinched at the mention of her name. "Oh Nathan, are you still obsessed with that woman? I thought we discussed this, that you understood how wrong she was for you."

Nathan shook his head. "Everything I believed in regards to her was based on a lie and it was a lie *he* handed over to me. Answer me, Father."

"What will you have me say," his father finally said, pushing to his feet on unsteady legs, although he waved his wife away when she moved to help him. He drew a few long breaths, leaning on the table, before he let his gaze move to Nathan. "Yes. I did give you a letter that night."

"One that was apparently forged. Did you arrange to have

it written? Were you responsible for that?" Nathan barked, slamming a fist down on the table.

His mother jumped at the unexpected violence, but his father did not react. He merely tilted his head slightly.

"Arthur!" his wife exclaimed, covering her lips with her fingers. "You forged a letter from Miss Willows?"

"It was the truth, in the end," the Marquis said slowly. "After all, the woman did become a mistress." He shot his wife an apologetic look. "A glorified whore, if you will pardon my coarseness, my dear. So what I had written there might not have been true that night, but it would have become true later. I had to make you see her character, one way or another."

Nathan clenched his fists at his sides. He was shaking so violently that his teeth clattered against each other in his mouth.

"Do you know what you did?" he managed to push out past his clenched jaw. "When I believed she had been untrue to me, I never considered any other reason behind her not showing up at our meeting place. I abandoned her when something horrible had kept her from me. And I . . ."

He trailed off and stared at his father as a new realization dawned upon him.

"If you had a forged letter ready for me, you must have believed Cassandra wouldn't come that night. That I would wait for her and when I came home, brokenhearted and angry, I would be open to your lies. How . . ." He could hardly say it. "How did you know Cassandra wouldn't meet me that night?"

His father blanched and swallowed hard enough that his Adam's apple bobbed in his throat.

"Why live in the past, Nathan?" he asked, his fists opening and closing against the tabletop before him. "What has been done has been done."

"How did you know, Father?" Nathan asked again. "What did you do?"

His father shot his mother a side glance, but she was staring at her husband with as much horror and anxiety as Nathan felt, himself. He couldn't help but be relieved that it seemed only one parent had been involved in the deceit.

"The bastard I hired was not supposed to attack her," his father said, lifting his hands as if for understanding.

Nathan shut his eyes, recoiling from his father's words like they were a physical blow. The pain that followed them certainly felt as powerful as a physical one.

"You knew what he did to her, you knew he raped her, and you never told me?" Nathan whispered, afraid that if he shouted he would never regain control over his voice or his actions. At this moment, he wasn't certain what he was capable of.

His mother got to her feet at that and spun on her husband with a gasp of pure dismay. "Arthur! *No*, you didn't. You didn't cause that poor woman to be attacked!"

When his father turned on his mother, the Marquis' face was pale as a ghost. "He was only supposed to hold her, Phillipa. I swear to you."

"But he didn't just hold her, did he, Father?"

Nathan was shocked that his tone was even remotely calm considering he had a powerful urge to throttle the man who had sired and raised him. A man he had loved.

"I wasn't responsible for what he did to her," his father said, his tone becoming defensive. "Whatever she told you, we came to terms. I paid her quite handsomely for her pain and trouble."

His mother hissed out a breath and paced away. Nathan watched her for a moment. It seemed she could empathize with Cassandra's experience, even if his father was trapped in denial and justification.

"Did you?" Nathan choked. "How much was that horrible experience worth to you, I wonder? As if your money could have ever erased what you did, what you caused."

His father shook his head. "Do you mean you didn't know?"

Nathan sighed. "No, my lord. Although Cassandra did confess tonight about the attack upon her, under great duress, she did not betray your actions. She protected you."

He moved for the door, unable to look at his father any longer. He was unable to face the past any longer and know that his part in it had been just as devastating to Cassandra as any other.

"She protected me," Nathan said softly. "Even though I have done nothing to deserve her consideration."

His father limped around the table, clinging to its edge as he did so. "You can speak to me in such dismissive terms, you can blame me for everything that happened four years ago, but there is something you must remember."

Nathan spun back, just barely reining in the violence of his anger, the nausea that boiled within him as he stared at the face of this . . . this *stranger*. "And what is that, Father?"

"I may have created the lie," his father said, a cough beginning to rise up between his words. "But you were quick to believe it, my boy. What does that tell you? What does that say?"

"Arthur!" his mother burst out, rushing across the room, to position herself between the two men. Clearly, she sensed her son's pure rage and his ability, at that moment, to forget that this frail man was his father.

But Nathan's rage was deflating. His father had said almost the exact same words that Cassandra had said earlier that night. And just as they had in that moment, they rang just as true now. In the end, the problems between him and Cassandra hadn't been created by his father or the lies. They had been created because Nathan hadn't had faith.

And as he walked away from his family home, he knew that was something he could never repair and never take back.

Chapter Seventeen

Cassandra watched as her maids folded her clothing, carefully placing it in trunk after trunk under her watchful eye. When the door behind her opened, she turned away from the servants and managed a weak smile as Elinor stepped into the room.

"I see you are almost finished here," her friend said, as she came to Cassandra's side and slipped an arm through hers.

Cassandra sighed as she rested her head on Elinor's shoulder. "I am, indeed. Only a few more things and I shall be ready to go to Bath for the remainder of the Season."

"I will miss you quite desperately," her friend said with a sad sigh. "But I truly believe this is the best course of action for you, my dear. You need the break away from London, from the matrons of the *ton* and from . . ."

Her friend trailed off and Cassandra's smile fell. "And from Nathan. You may say his name, I will not shatter."

It had been a week since she had seen him, since she had poured her pain out to him. In that time, her only contact with him had been a brief note that only said, "I'm sorry."

She had it in her pelisse pocket where she could touch it whenever she desired.

"I know you won't," her friend said softly. "You are too strong to shatter."

Cassandra shrugged one shoulder. She could debate that point with her friend if she had the energy. But instead, she said, "This 'break,' as you call it, may be good for me, but it will wreak havoc on my business. I shall likely lose many customers to other seamstresses. And the customers who desire my toys . . ."

Elinor laughed. "Will order them through normal means and wait the extra time it takes for you to send them back to London if they need them desperately."

"I suppose," Cassandra conceded with a sigh.

Her friend patted her hand. "I have put a great deal of thought into the matter since you told me you wanted to leave the city and I actually think this time away could make you even more sought after. The upper class always wants what they cannot have more than what is right in front of them. They sometimes break embargoes in the name of fashion, why would they not travel to Bath?"

Cassandra shrugged. "Perhaps."

"At any rate, I shall make sure that the gowns you finished are delivered. And when orders for toys come in from the gentlemen, I will be here to forward the information on to you and collect their money." Elinor smiled. "You may depend upon me."

"I always have," Cassandra said, touching her friend's cheek. Then she let her hands flutter down around her waist. She smoothed her skirt restlessly. "But there is one more thing to discuss. If Nathan does come here—"

"He shall not hear where you are from me," Elinor said, her expression turning angry and sour. "No one shall."

"Not even me?"

Both women turned as Stephan Undercliffe strode into the bedchamber with a wide smile. He took off his hat and gave the women a bow. Relief flooded Cassandra. Since the day when he had almost confessed his true feelings for her, they had not spent time together. She actually feared that their old friendship had been irrevocably damaged. But seeing him, his easy smile just as it had always been and his eyes sparkling with mischief, not sadness or regret, she was put at ease.

"Of course *you* shall know where I am," she teased. "I was about to write you a note to tell you my direction in Bath in case you came to take the waters later in the Season."

"Ah, yes, the curative waters." Stephan winked. "*Delicious.*"

She laughed for the first time in days at his comment. The waters of Bath were as known for their terrible taste as they were for their supposed healing powers.

Then he grew serious. "Do you think I might have a moment with you in private, Cassandra?"

She couldn't help but stiffen slightly, yet he had always been a good friend to her. She couldn't deny him this. She nodded toward the servants still buzzing about her chamber.

"Please go to my workroom and begin packing there." She tilted her head toward Elinor. "Will you oversee that?"

Elinor nodded and gave Stephan a brief smile. "Of course."

Once they were alone, Stephan's smile faded a fraction. "The waters do not cure a broken heart, you know."

She flinched. "Am I so obvious?"

"Only to one who knows the truth," he reassured her, as he reached out to squeeze her hand. "Since Lord Blackhearth did not arrive on my doorstep demanding satisfaction, I assume you never told him that you and I had renewed our 'affiliation.' Are you running away from London as an alternative?"

Cassandra laughed bitterly. "I did tell him. He did not believe me."

"I am wounded," Stephan chuckled, though the sound was gentle, not mocking. "He did not believe my charms to be irresistible to you?"

She shrugged. "Shocking, I realize. Actually, it truly *was* a shock to me. Years ago, he was willing to think the worst of me, upon only hearsay. But when he heard the same from my own lips, he would not take it as fact."

She frowned. And it hadn't been guilt that had made him disbelieve she would be untrue. She had told him about Stephan *before* she revealed the truth about the attack upon her.

Stephan seemed to consider that for a long while. "Perhaps

the man has changed," he offered. "Perhaps he has faith now. Faith in you and in what you share."

She shivered. How many times had she wished for such a thing in the time they had been parted? But now . . . it was terrifying.

"Are you certain you want to walk away? It is clear that leaving London, leaving this man, pains you greatly." He touched her cheek. "I hate to see it."

"This is what needs to happen," she whispered, moving away from his touch to pace around her nearly empty room. She kept hoping if she said those words enough times, she would believe them.

Stephan made no move to follow her as she paced. "Yes, but it is difficult to get what we need when it isn't what we truly want."

"You are a good friend," she mused, smiling at him as she turned back. "I hope that never changes."

She saw his smile falter just a fraction. "It never will."

With a shake of her head, she forced herself to lighten her mood. "I have no time to talk nonsense with you, Mr. Undercliffe. I have much to do to prepare for my journey."

His brow wrinkled with concern and she came to him with the brightest smile she could manage. "Do not fret over me, dearest Stephan. I shall go to Bath, and I shall take the waters, and I shall forget."

He stroked a finger over her cheekbone. "You shall not forget, Cass. But I hope you will be happy."

She held back a sob as his arms came around her and he hugged her. Not as a former lover, not as a man who had feelings she could never return . . . but as her friend. And she clung to him as she tried to ignore how true his words were.

When Stephan Undercliffe strode into Nathan's private room at his club and slammed the door in the face of the exquisitely liveried servant who was chasing him, Nathan could do nothing to mask his utter surprise. After their brief encounter at the Whipplesham soiree, and after Cassandra tried to convince him that the two had become lovers again, he hadn't expected to see Undercliffe.

And yet now Cassandra's former lover stood before Nathan with his arms folded, glaring daggers into him. Quietly, he folded his paper and set it on the small table beside his leather chair. He hoped his curiosity was not as evident to the other man as it was to him.

"Good afternoon, Undercliffe," he drawled. "I don't recall asking you to join me, but I do have some excellent scotch here and a few fine cigars."

"I don't want your damn liquor," Undercliffe snapped, his normally wickedly playful expression surprisingly serious. "I came here to tell you that you are a fucking idiot of the highest order and you should be drawn and quartered for what you've done to Cassandra."

Nathan winced. It had been a fortnight since he spoke to Cassandra. How many times had he gotten on his horse and headed for her home, only to stop himself? A dozen? A hundred? A thousand? He ached to see her, to hold her, to talk to her . . . but she had asked him to let her go.

And the very least he could do was follow that directive.

"The blackmail you mean?" he asked dully, taking a huge swig of his stale drink. "Yes, I think we've established that I'm a horrible, terrible man. But that is over. She has nothing left to fear."

"Not the blackmail, you sapscull!" Undercliffe strode to the opposite side of the room and glared at him. "I'm talking about letting her go."

"Letting her go? Where has she gone?" Nathan asked, rising to his feet.

Undercliffe looked at Nathan like he had lit a fire on the crown of his own head. "She went to Bath three days ago. She left London. The way she behaved before she went, she might never return."

Nathan collapsed back into the chair with a sharp exhalation of breath. His chest ached. She was gone. He would never accidentally encounter her at his aunt's, or see her on the street, or be able to pass by her window and peek in on her again.

"It is . . ." He shook his head. "It is for the best. I hurt her. I believed the worst of her when she had never given me any indication that she wasn't to be believed. And indirectly or not, I caused something horrible to happen to her."

Undercliffe wrinkled his brow in confusion and Nathan

leaned back in his chair. The other man didn't know the whole story. It was just as well, for he would probably try to kill Nathan if he knew what Cassandra had been through. Not that he didn't deserve that and worse.

"She asked me to leave her alone," Nathan finished with a sigh. "The best I can do for her now is to do that. Perhaps she will be happy in Bath."

Undercliffe stared at him before he grabbed for the fine bottle of scotch and poured himself a tall drink of it. As he sat down in a seat across from Nathan, he shook his head.

"You know what your problem is, your lordship? It's that you are nothing more than a spoiled, titled infant."

Both Nathan's eyebrows came up. He had been called many things in his life, but never that. He didn't know whether to be offended or to laugh.

"I beg your pardon?"

Undercliffe took a sip of his scotch and his eyes went wide when he tasted the high quality alcohol. He lifted his glass before he said, "I think you heard me perfectly damn well. You have been given everything you ever wanted your entire life. You never had to work or fight or sacrifice for anything. But with Cassandra, it is different. And yet, despite the fact that she is a jewel amongst women and you don't deserve to *look* at her, let alone love her, you still aren't willing to fight. To sacrifice for her."

He snorted his disgust.

Nathan stared at the man even harder. "And you know all

this because you know me so well," he said, dry. Although despite his attitude the things this man was saying actually rang true. Not that he would give Undercliffe the satisfaction of admitting that.

"Trust me, I know you. I grew up with a man exactly like you." Undercliffe shook his head and downed the rest of his drink. "My older brother never had to earn anything either and he still doesn't. Being titled doesn't make you wise or good, that is for certain. It just makes you rich and pompous."

"That may be true," Nathan admitted finally with a shrug. "But trust me that it is a sacrifice to stay away from Cassandra. It kills me to follow her bidding."

"Do forgive me if I don't grant you a medal for your honor," Undercliffe snorted. "I saw Cassandra before she departed for Bath and she is miserable without you."

"What?" Nathan breathed, a faint flicker of hope awakening inside of him.

Undercliffe rolled his eyes like Nathan was daft. "You are honoring the wrong request, you dolt. I'm sure somewhere in the past you two share, she asked you to love her."

Nathan nodded, assaulted by his memories of a younger Cassandra, untouched by tragedy, giving herself to him so freely, telling him she loved him, and asking him if he could ever love her, even though they lived such different lives.

"Then honor that request. Love her. Go to her. *Fight*, maybe for the first time in your pampered life. Lower yourself, offer her anything she desires, give her everything she deserves. Do whatever you have to do."

Nathan blinked. "Obviously you care deeply for Cassandra. Why would you suggest that I go to her if you think she desires me? Why not take advantage of this situation, yourself?"

The fire left the other man's stare in an instant. "Because I do love her. And she loves you. I want her to be happy and you are the one who will do that if you drag your sorry head out of your sorrier ass."

Nathan dipped his chin. Here was a man willing to make the ultimate sacrifice just to see Cassandra happy. It shamed him, yet again, to think that he hadn't been ready to go so far. But he was now. And he would make it up to her for the rest of her life if she would allow him to speak.

"I owe you an apology," Nathan said, as he moved for the door. "When we met I hated that you had been something to Cassandra. I hated that you had ever touched her. But you are obviously a good friend to her. You helped her when she was broken, and you healed her when I was too foolish to do the same. So I owe you a great deal."

Undercliffe seemed surprised, but he got to his feet nonetheless. "You can make it up to me by loving her. And you have to go all the way. She can't just be your lover, your mistress. Because my honorable tendencies only go so far. If I feel you aren't doing the right thing when it comes to her, I will step in. And I will find a way to have her myself."

Nathan swallowed. The idea of that made him want to put a hole in this man's head with his fist. But he understood why Undercliffe said it. He even respected it in some way.

"If you come near my *future wife*," he responded, putting just the right emphasis on his words. "I will make you sorry."

"Then we understand each other," Undercliffe said with a sad smile.

.Nathan nodded. "Good day. I have a great deal to do before I depart for Bath."

Chapter Eighteen

Cassandra stared out the open breakfast room window down onto the small garden behind the townhome she had let in Bath. It was nothing compared to her one at home, but she had enjoyed the hours she had spent tending it since her arrival. She drew in a deep breath of fresh air and let it out in a long sigh.

Bath was beautiful, its naturally warm springwaters were everything that had been said about them. And Cassandra had been the toast of the small Society there since her arrival. Women who could not make it to London for her gowns had been begging her to design something for them, throwing amounts of money at her that made her head spin.

But she had turned them all down, opting instead to rest. Relax. But that strategy was swiftly backfiring. Without work and her small but close circle of friends as a blessed distraction, Cassandra's loneliness had begun to feel stifling and overpowering.

Even when she was out in the small, middle-class society of Bath, dancing and meeting new friends, she didn't feel a part of the gaiety. Not when her heart was breaking.

Before she could become too maudlin, the door to the chamber opened and her new butler stepped inside. He gave her a brief, apologetic bow before he said, "I beg your pardon, Miss Willows, but you have a visitor."

Her eyebrows arched in surprise. "So early?"

The servant nodded, his expression just as exhausted by the idea as her own.

It was only nine in the morning, and the one thing she had learned about the people in Bath, it was that they kept the same lazy hours as those in London. She sighed as she silently prayed her guest was not one of the pushy women bent on having a "Cassandra Willows Creation" made and made this very moment. Although she might begin to work here and there while she visited the small city, she wasn't ready to create yet. She hadn't felt creative since . . .

"Send the person in," she said, cutting off her thoughts. "If they have come here at such an early hour, their mission must be of no-doubt great importance."

As the butler left the room to fetch the intruder, Cassandra got up and went to the china hutch across from the door. She fetched a teacup and saucer for her guest. There was no reason not to be polite, even if she didn't want to see anyone.

She began to turn as the butler reappeared. He opened his mouth to announce the visitor when the man stepped around him and into her view.

Cassandra almost dropped the cup when she saw that it was no unwanted stranger at all who had invaded upon her privacy, but Nathan. Nathan standing in front of her gaping servant. Nathan with dark circles beneath his bright eyes, with his hands shaking ever so slightly as he gripped his hat in white-knuckled fingers.

"Nathan," she breathed, rather stupidly, but it was the only thing she could think to say.

"Hello, Cass," he whispered in return.

The servant immediately recognized he was not wanted and backed away without further word.

"I realize you asked me not to bother you again," he said as he reached behind him and closed the door. "But I needed to see you." He hesitated. "I wanted so much to see you."

She shut her eyes, still clinging to the cup that dangled from her fingertips. "I see."

She motioned him further into the room. "Since you have come so far, why don't you come in? I can see no harm in our talking if it is that important to you."

No harm except for her aching heart, of course. No doubt it would take her weeks to recover from seeing him again. At this rate, she would never get over him.

Nathan moved forward just a step, almost as if he were afraid to come closer.

"Your—your home here is very lovely," he stammered.

She couldn't help but smile at his broken attempts at small talk. Apparently this situation wasn't any easier for him than it was for her.

"Thank you," she said. "It is not my home, but I do like it." She tilted her head. "Is that why you came here? To inspect my new abode?"

"You know it isn't," he whispered. "Cass, I can understand why you wanted to keep the pain of your attack private, especially from me. I gave you no reason to trust me with such a secret."

He flinched, and the true and real guilt in his stare made her heart ache.

"Part of why I didn't tell you was because I knew you would torment yourself, just as you are doing now," she said softly, coming toward him. She deposited the cup on the table and moved to him, taking his hands in hers and squeezing gently. "What happened that night was not your fault. I may have blamed you for your reaction afterward, but I never blamed you for the actions of that man."

He was staring at their interlocked fingers, his breathing slightly labored. When he lifted that shocking blue gaze to hers, she could not look away. Being so close to him again when she had never thought she would, feeling the warmth of his breath on her skin and the intensity of his stare on her face . . . those things were like sensual witchcraft, weaving a spell around her.

"What about the actions of my father?" he whispered. "Did you ever blame me for those?"

She sucked in her breath sharply. She had prayed this day would never come. Even in her darkest moments, she hadn't wanted Nathan to know what his father had done. How he had caused all the pain that had broken her life into shards. How he had thought that paying her money would be a salve for a gaping wound.

"How did you find out?" she asked, extracting her hands from his and pacing away.

Nathan moved into the room a few more steps and sighed with the weight of the world in the sound. "Part of the reason I believed you had abandoned me on that night all those years ago was because my father gave me a letter supposedly written by you. One that detailed your plans to throw me over for another man."

Cassandra gasped as she faced him.

A letter? She had never known about that part of the treachery his father had set in motion that night. His father had made it clear that only a word from him had turned Nathan against her. But if Nathan had seen some kind of *proof* that she had abandoned him, especially after a humiliating night of waiting for her, it made more sense that he might have believed the worst.

Nathan continued, "Once you told me what truly happened to you, I realized that letter must have been a forgery. I had hoped that my father wasn't involved, but once I confronted him . . . well . . ."

He hesitated and his expression darkened with a potent mixture of anger, sadness, and disappointment.

"The truth came out," she finished for him softly.

He nodded.

She smiled sadly. "It has a way of doing that."

He looked at her, holding her captive with just his stare. "I wish you had told me about his part in all this. That my own father sent the man who attacked you to keep you away from me, and that he paid you off once he realized what the bastard had done to you."

She nodded. "Perhaps I should have."

"Why didn't you?" he asked. "Did you not think I deserved to know?"

"Oh, Nathan," she sighed. "It wasn't about keeping something from you out of spite. I just . . . I couldn't stand the thought of you hating your father. Of you seeing him in such an ugly light."

He stared at her, his face filled with shock. "I am in awe of you, Cassandra. He is the last person in the world who deserves your concern."

She thought about that for a long moment. How could she explain the peace which had only come to her after years of anger?

"Your father and I never got along, but I believed him when he said that he never meant for me to be raped or harmed in any physical way that night. He was wrong." Her voice elevated even when she didn't intend it to. "*Very wrong* and I shall never forget what he did to me. But I have forgiven him. And not because he paid me, but because I realized that if I held on to the hatred of the man who hurt me, or the hatred of your father . . . it would only scar *me*. I realized that in order to move on, I had to put those angry, hurt feelings away and find a way to be happy again. It was part of why I became a mistress when I came to London."

He tilted his head. "After what happened to you—"

She lifted a hand to interrupt him. "I couldn't let one man's violence destroy my view of myself, of sex, or of men in general. I wouldn't let myself be permanently maimed by him. I'm not saying it was easy, but over time and with very good and gentle men as my guide, I was able to move on."

He nodded slowly.

With a sigh, she said, "Once I began to heal, I didn't want to hurt anyone else as I had been hurt. And I knew that if I told you what he had done, it would devastate the relationship you have with him. And I wouldn't have done that to you. I know you love your father and I never would have been party to destroying your image of him. It isn't as if my doing so would have changed the past."

Nathan shook his head slowly. "You are so good, Cass. So much better than anyone I have ever known. If you hated him, hated me, railed at the world, worked to destroy my entire family . . . no one would blame you. *I* wouldn't blame you. And yet what you did was gather up what he broke, what that bastard who hurt you broke, and made a new life."

He hesitated and looked away. "Until I came back and forced you to return to unhappy times. I forced you as much as the man who raped you."

Without thinking, without considering the consequences,

Cassandra marched across the room. She cupped Nathan's cheeks with both hands and tilted his face so that he looked directly at her.

"Listen to me, Nathan, hear me. I may have struggled against what you were demanding, but if I had not wanted this . . . wanted you . . . I would have found a way around it. Never compare yourself to that . . . that *person* ever again. You *never* forced me to do anything I do not want with all my heart."

He stared at her, his gaze so focused and heated that she flushed. Slowly his hands came up and he cupped her elbows. His body asked her permission with every slow, subtle move. And she was too weak not to grant it.

"You *do* want me with all your heart, sweet?" he asked, his mouth descending with aching slowness. "Or you did once?"

She should resist him. It wasn't fair to either one of them to allow him to kiss her or touch her or make love to her. But standing there, his breath hot on her lips, his arms coming around her in a gentle embrace, she couldn't find the strength to deny him.

And when he kissed her, she lost all control. She opened to him, gliding her tongue out to taste him, pulling him close to feel the warmth of his hard chest against hers, to tangle her legs with his. She had been without him for over four years and yet the last two weeks had felt like an eternity.

She needed one more good memory. One more unforgettable encounter to erase the pain of her confession the last time they were together. Then it would be enough. *Then* she could let him go forever.

Except he pulled back, panting. Staring down at her, he gasped out, "I don't want to force you, I don't want to hurt—"

She didn't let him finish, but lifted her fingers to cover his lips. "Don't treat me like glass, Nathan. Touch me like you want to touch me. And know that if I didn't want you, if I didn't want anything, I would let you know."

She grasped his hand and lifted it, covering her breast with a groan of pleasure. "Touch me. Fill me. Make me tremble. *That* is what I want."

He bit out a curse before he dropped his mouth to hers again. She sighed as the hesitation she had sensed in him fled, replaced by an urgency that mirrored her own.

Although this hadn't been his plan when he came here, Nathan couldn't fight the intense need to be with Cassandra any more than he could fight the need to breathe or blink. And now that he had her permission to take, to claim, to be with her, he wasn't about to back away. Not unless she said no.

And she didn't say no. In fact, when he guided her back toward the table and pushed her up against the edge, she let out a low moan of pure pleasure that seemed to echo in the charged air around them. He buried his lips into her throat, sucking at the tender skin there, smiling as she jolted against him. Her breasts flattened against his chest and her hips pounded against his as the table rattled behind her.

He found the buttons along the front of her gown and loosened them, peeling open the silken fabric and pulling down the chemise beneath. Then he leaned back and looked at her.

Morning light was coming in from the windows that faced out over a well-tended garden. It cascaded over her pale body, making her glow, making her utterly luminous. Her heavy, full breasts were flushed with desire, the small, pink nipples already swollen and dark. When he touched them, he could see that she would go wild. She was so sensitive, she might even come.

She might not allow this again, they had not yet made any promises. So if he was going to make love to her now, he had to make it a seduction. A promise of a future. A way to beg her to let him stay with her, even though he didn't deserve such a boon.

In short, he had to please her like she had never been pleased before.

That was a challenge he was more than willing to meet and he returned his lips to her throat, sucking hard on her skin until she cried out in ecstasy. He inched down, bracing his weight on the table as his glided his tongue over the peak of her collarbone, lower to the swell of her breasts.

When he finally reached her nipples, he cupped her breasts, lifting, gently pressing them together. She moaned a needy, incoherent sound as she flopped her head back. He licked lazily across the swell, moving toward her nipples, but never quite suckling them. With every teasing graze of his tongue, Cassandra's moans intensified, her head thrashed back and forth, and her fingers clenched against the table behind her.

"Please," she finally moaned, lifting her head to look at him. "Please, please Nathan."

He could hardly resist her begging. Keeping his gaze locked with hers, he smoothed his lips over her nipple and sucked. She bucked against him with a groan. Her body was shaking, rattling the dishes on the table behind her. She was so close to release. So close that he could scent her arousal.

He pushed her skirts up with one hand, utterly lacking in finesse but filled with undeniable passion. He cupped her smooth skin, sliding his hand up until he found the wet folds of her pussy. As he sucked at her turgid nipple, he spread her outer lips and ground his thumb down over the harsh ridge of her already aroused clit.

She exploded, wet heat flowing over his fingers, her body slamming against his as she rode out a powerful orgasm. He throbbed as he watched her find her pleasure, his cock hard enough to pound nails if he so desired.

But he wasn't going to take her yet, no matter how much he wanted to. No, this joining was about her. Making her come. Making her remember that she needed him. First physically, then emotionally. He wanted to open her to him in every way that was important.

If he wanted a chance to be with her—to love her—for more than just this one day, that was the only way.

Her body quivered a few more times and then she went limp against him. He held her for a few moments, smoothing her auburn hair and rubbing his hands down her spine.

Finally, she lifted her chin and smiled at him. "The things you do to me, Nathan Manning . . ."

He grinned in return. "And I'm not finished yet."

Her eyes went wide, but before she could reply, he dropped to his knees before her. Perched on the edge of the breakfast table with her skirts already piled up around her hips and her legs spread from his fingers, she was in perfect position.

"Nathan," she said, her tone a question and a warning at once.

He ignored her plea and instead grabbed for the chocolate croissant that she had left, half eaten from her breakfast. The rocking of her hips had knocked the pastry to the edge of the table. He gave her a wicked smile.

"You are already sweet, Cass," he said, swirling his finger through the melted chocolate and coating the digit. "But I want you sweeter."

Cassandra gasped as Nathan shouldered his way between her legs. When he stroked his chocolaty finger across her already soaked slit, her quim quivered. God, he felt so good. Her clit was still swollen and achy, her sheath still clenching in tiny earthquakes from the prior release. Just the faintest touch, just the idea that he was coating her with sweet chocolate to make her a tasty treat, was enough to make her clench and sigh with pleasure.

He looked up and her sigh turned to a moan. What a wicked picture he made, kneeling between her spread thighs, smoothing his finger back and forth across her pussy like a painter with his masterpiece. He lifted it to his mouth and touched his tongue to the tip.

"Delicious," he murmured. "Want to try it?"

She nodded, mesmerized by his seductive voice. He lifted his hand and she let him trace her lips before she sucked his finger into her mouth. She laved her tongue around him, pretending it was his cock as she licked the earthly mixture of chocolate and her juices away.

Reluctantly, he pulled his finger away with a low moan. "Fight fair, sweet. I'm not finished with you yet; don't make me think of things you can't have."

"I could have them if I wanted," she said, arching back and letting him get a good look at her bare breasts, her spread legs. He shivered, and triumph filled her.

"You could, but you won't," he chuckled before he lowered his head and she felt him suck her clit into his mouth.

She bucked at the focused, hard pressure. He swirled his tongue around her, licking her clean, tormenting her beyond measure and reason. She let go of the edge of the table and glided her fingers into his hair. He laughed against her slit as she angled him closer, but he didn't resist her silent orders and drove his tongue deeper inside her clenching body. Her hips ground against him, pushing him further inside, milking him as he teased and toyed with her pussy.

And then, the world went silent, all her focus going to the sweet spot between her legs. To his tongue, to the way his fingers dug into her thighs as he held her steady. Pleasure spiraled up, hot and wicked, and she quivered out of control with an orgasm so powerful that she couldn't focus on anything but the pleasure.

He licked at her through every shiver, every moment of release, dragging the ecstasy out until she could hardly bear it. She was weak with it, spent as she sagged against the table and his shoulders.

Nathan stood slowly, remaining wedged between her thighs. She whimpered when he gently slid her arms away, but the sound faded when he began to divest himself of his clothing with silent determination. His shirt fell away, revealing his tanned chest, lightly peppered with a little hair across the broad muscles.

His trousers went next, sliding away from toned, narrow hips into a pile, which he kicked away. His cock was hard, swollen, and curved against his flat abdomen.

"You said I did things to you," he panted, stepping back into position against her. She groaned as his cock rubbed her belly. "But feel what you do to me."

She didn't have to be asked twice. Still watching his face, she gripped his cock, stroking it from base to head in a smooth motion. His eyelids fluttered shut and she almost crowed in triumph. How she loved moving him, bringing him pleasure. It had always been her favorite pastime.

And even if this encounter between them was just fantasy, she had no intention of halting it. Not when he was so close. Not when she could have a final taste of passion and pleasure unlike any she'd ever known.

She cupped the back of his neck with her free hand and tugged until their foreheads touched. Their breath mingled and moved in time as she stroked him over and over.

"More," he groaned, and suddenly he was edging closer, lifting her ever so slightly to position himself against her ready opening.

With a gasp that she wasn't sure was her own or his, he slid home deep within her body. She clung to him, their heads still touching, their eyes locked. She readied for him to move, but he didn't. He only held inside her, filling her and *feeling* her.

"You are mine, Cassandra Willows," he whispered. "Say that you are mine."

She shook her head. "It's not fair."

"Say it anyway," he murmured and flexed inside of her.

She groaned and nodded. "I'm yours. You are mine."

He smiled and thrust gently. They held each other close, keeping their eyes locked. She slipped her hands through his hair and watched his pupils dilate, hold hers with that startling intensity that had always unnerved her.

Now, watching him while he took her was a whole new experience. Far more intense. Far more meaningful. They rocked together at first lazy and slow, but as their pelvises ground against each other, as her clit rubbed against him perfectly, her excitement grew. Their hips met faster, their bodies thrust with more purpose. The pleasure mounted deep within her, with tingles starting just at her clit and slowly spreading with warm pleasure throughout her body.

Nathan felt her orgasm approaching when her spine stiffened. She arched up with a cry and shuddered through a third orgasm. He held her steady, his mouth still close to hers without kissing her, his fingers cupping her hips as he thrust and retreated, over and over. He wanted to make the moment last, to lengthen the sweet torment.

But her cries and jerky movements affected him. He swelled inside her, his driving hips moving more urgently and out of control. It was a war he couldn't win, so with a guttural cry, he came within her, slamming her against the table's edge with every final thrust and finally relaxing against her with a moan of completion.

For a long time they stayed that way. Although their bodies were still joined, Nathan felt Cassandra drifting away from him. Fading back to that place where she could say that this moment was just a fleeting weakness, not something that could last forever.

He had to get her back.

"We shouldn't have done that," she whispered, resting her forehead on his shoulder as she clung to him.

"No," he agreed, nuzzling the side of her neck until she shivered delicately. "You see, I promised myself I wouldn't make love to you again until you were my wife."

She stiffened and for a long moment she didn't move. But finally, almost reluctantly, she lifted her face and stared at him.

"Your wife?" she repeated on what could hardly be called a whisper.

He nodded, though his heart was throbbing so fast and strong that he feared he might lose consciousness. "I didn't come here to talk to you about the past, you see. We needed to do that, of course, but that wasn't my motive. And it wasn't to make love to you on your breakfast table, as spectacular an experience as that was. I came here to tell you that I want to marry you. Still. Always. If you will have me. Will you have me, Cassandra?"

Chapter Nineteen

If Cassandra hadn't been so utterly aware of every minute thing around her, she might have thought this was a dream. After all, she had visited this very moment while sleeping a dozen times or more. It was all so familiar—Nathan returning to her, him still wanting to be her husband, even though so much had happened. In her dreams, she fell into his arms and they lived happily ever after.

But that was a fantasy! Something that she could wish for, but never have. There were too many obstacles for it to work. Too much history.

She shook her head, though it was difficult to do so. "You know I cannot," she whispered, shifting so their bodies separated and lowering her feet to the floor. She pressed her hands against his warm chest gently. "*You* cannot."

"I just did," he reminded her, seemingly not put off at all by her refusal. In fact, he was smiling at her, indulgent, as though he knew convincing her would only be a matter of time.

She feared he might be right.

"This is a daydream, Nathan," she sighed, smoothing her wrinkled skirt back down over her hips and trying to untwist the bodice so she could slip her arms into the sleeves. "Nothing more than fancy after the heat of making love. There are too many things between us."

"The past?" he asked, his tanned face losing some of its color as he watched her dress.

She fastened her buttons with clumsy fingers. "Yes, but not in the way you believe. As I said, I made peace with everything that happened to me. I refused to let what happened to me rule my life. That was why I took your father's money, that was why I came to London and began my business. It's why I became the mistress of those men. All those things gave me control over my life. And they helped me to remember that a man's touch could be good."

Nathan shook his head. "In some strange way, I thank those men for giving you that gift, but damn it, Cass, it should have been me."

She took his hand briefly. "Regrets are dangerous things, Nathan. We shouldn't live with them, they will destroy us. Here is what we shall do. First, you will forgive yourself for the actions that *other people* took without your knowledge or your blessing."

He sighed, but she could see her words had an effect. And

perhaps that was all she could give him. It had to be enough.

"Next," she continued, "we will celebrate the fact that regardless of the circumstances, we were brought back together in London. And I do not regret anything about the passion we shared."

Even falling in love, though she couldn't say that out loud, for it would only encourage his reckless folly in asking her to marry him again. If he did that too many times, she might succumb to her weakness and agree.

"Nothing?" he asked, grabbing his trousers from the floor and stepping into them.

He didn't fasten them, so they hung low on his hips. Her mouth went dry as she looked at him, his dark hair tousled from her fingers. His lips were red and swollen from kissing her all over. There was a thin sheen of sweat on his muscles. He looked good enough to eat. Good enough to love for the rest of her life.

She forced herself to look away as she fixed her hair in the mirror across the room.

"I regret nothing, it costs too much," she repeated with difficulty. "But that changes nothing. So the last thing we shall do is . . ."

She turned back. He deserved to be faced when she said this, no matter how hard it was to do it.

"We shall realize that this is not something we can continue."

He opened his mouth, but she held up her hand and he shut it.

"Nathan, you must see all the obstacles that separate us. Your parents' continued disapproval will always be an issue, and then there is the detail of our insurmountable variance in social and financial status. The fact that I am in *trade* alone will cause problems that you may not have considered."

"I have thought about this far more than you give me credit for," he said quietly.

She shook her head with a little shiver. "If you have, then you must know it could never work. When I agreed to marry you all those years ago, I was young and naïve. I believed we could overcome any resistance to our love. That somehow we could convince the world that it was good and right. But I have been on the edge of your Society for many years now. I have seen them eat their *own* alive for some minor transgression. They will never accept me. It would be a nightmare for us, as well as any children we might bring into the world."

To her surprise, Nathan's face broke into a wide, faraway smile. She frowned.

"The idea of the torment makes you happy?"

He shook his head, coming back to her. "No, of course not. But I was just picturing the beautiful children you and I would create. Picturing you as a mother."

Tears stung at Cassandra's eyes. Once she had glorious dreams about bearing this man's sons and daughters. She had been able to picture those children so clearly that they were almost real to her. Over time, she had tried to forget that, but now her own words had forced her to remember.

"You could be the mother of my child right now," he whispered in that coaxing tone before he came forward and pressed a hand to the low curve of her belly. "We have not been careful every time. Including today."

She shivered and tried to tamp down the joy that accompanied that observation. "Was that by design? To force my hand?"

He shook his head. "Not at all. When I started my blackmail, I had every intention of being very careful when I made love to you. I was so angry, so misguided and stupid, that I wanted to pretend that I could have you without forging a bond. That in the end, I could discard you as I believed you had discarded me all those years ago."

He slid his hand up the apex of her body. She shivered when his palm glided between the valley of her breasts before he settled it against her cheek.

"But I think in my heart, I knew what would really happen."

"What?" she whispered.

He smiled. That knowing, certain smile that thrilled and terrified her all at once. "That I would fall in love with you."

Her eyes fluttered shut. Those were the most beautiful words in the world coming from the lips of the man she wanted to say them most. But for the good of them both, she was still driven to deny their power.

"But is it love, Nathan?"

He nodded. "You have every reason to doubt that. What you said, what my father said . . . you were both right. All those years ago, I turned away from you so quickly, so easily, it wasn't love that moved me. Not lasting love. But I'm not the same man that I was before, Cass. When you told me you wanted Undercliffe, I didn't believe you. I knew in my heart that you wouldn't betray me. I found the faith I lacked as a stupid, spoiled boy."

"Oh, Nathan," she breathed. Her walls were crumbling swiftly now and she fought to keep them up.

He made it more difficult by grasping her hands. "I lost you before. And it wasn't because you didn't show up the night of our rendezvous. It wasn't because of my father's machinations. *I* lost you through my actions. *My* failures. But you must know that the moment I saw you again in my aunt's house in London, I knew somewhere deep inside that I couldn't go a day without touching you. And I still can't. And not just touching you, but being with you. Near you. Seeing you smile. Making you laugh."

"But—"

Now it was he who interrupted her with a raised hand. "I know all the things you said to me, all those obstacles you listed . . . they are true. Society is fickle. They could easily see our love as some kind of fairytale, but it is more likely they will see it as a scandal. We won't be invited places. And, yes, our children may very well struggle because of our choices. But you told me not a moment ago that you wouldn't let the past rule your life. Are you willing to throw away the love I know you feel for me because of a *future* that may or may not come to pass?"

Cassandra drew back, looking up at him with wide eyes. He was making sense, too much sense. When he threw her own vows back at her, when he admitted his wrongdoings and responsibility, it made her believe in whatever he said.

It made her believe in him.

He looked at her. "You love me. And I love you. I see how you have overcome the past and I am so proud to love a woman who is so strong. But don't push your regrets into the future. I think we both know that anything can happen, for good or for bad. And I'm not willing to lose you again . . . not because of things that *might* happen. Are you? Are you truly?"

Her tears were becoming too strong to just blink away so Cassandra let them fall, sliding down her cheeks in hot trails as she stared at this man who held her so gently, so lovingly.

"No," she whispered.

He laughed, though the sound was slightly strained. "Is that a no, you don't want to throw away love. Or no, you still won't marry me."

"I—I don't want to throw away love," she whispered and as she said it, a great joy filled her. A relief. Her fears faded away and all that was left was happiness and light.

His hands tightened on her and his smile widened. In that moment, she saw the boy she had once loved. But she also saw the man she loved now. The one who had changed and grown in the time that had separated them. And though she couldn't be happy for those circumstances, perhaps that was the gift they had given her.

They were different people now. Wiser. Better suited. More willing to compromise and grow together.

"So, you will marry me?" he whispered.

She nodded. "I will marry you."

He let out a shout of joy before his mouth came down on hers. She clung to him, reveling in his love and in the love she returned to him. When he pulled away, she leaned in, wanting more.

"Will you run away with me right now to Gretna Green?" he asked, his eyes twinkling. "And then come with me to India?"

Her eyes widened. "Gretna Green? India!"

"I want to be with you *now*. Forget what my family thinks, forget what anyone else says. I don't give a fuck. I want to be with you. And I want to show you India, Cass. I want you to see all the things I wished I could show you when I was there. Please."

She nodded. How could she refuse?

"Gretna Green and India it is," she laughed, moving to go to the door. "I shall have my things packed straight away."

But before she could go, he pulled her back, wrapping her in his arms. "Wait, there is one more thing I want."

She smiled. "And what is that, my lord?"

"I'm still hungry. What say we make good work of those strawberries there?" he whispered, his voice low and seductive against her ear.

She tilted her face and kissed him as her answer. And as he guided her back to the table, she couldn't help but surrender everything she had and everything she was to the love of her life.

Jason Manning was three and he acted it as he raced across the sprawling country lawn toward his mother. He was crying out in a foreign language, speaking words of war and conquering.

Cassandra laughed as she watched her son take over the small village in his mind, then turned her attention back to her husband. They were sitting at a table on the terrace of their country estate in Bath, sharing breakfast.

Nathan grinned at his son and then reached out to touch her face. They had been away from England for nearly four years and she could see that being back was a pleasure for her husband, though their reasons for returning had been sad ones.

"At least you saw your father before he passed," she said

quietly, lifting her hand to cover his. "I am glad you made your peace with him. It was far past time."

"Yes," Nathan agreed softly. "And my mother has been accepting, as have my sisters. My aunt has even spoken in favor of our marriage. The fact that they are planning a party as soon as the mourning period is over to welcome you into our family will speak volumes to the *ton*."

"You mean the half who have not yet accepted me," Cassandra said, keeping an eye on Jason.

He took a tumble down the hill, then righted himself, rubbed his elbow absently, and went immediately back to whatever race he was running in his mind. She admired that childlike ability to overcome little pains.

"Indeed," Nathan said with a proud smile. "Years ago, I told you that Society would either view our marriage as a scandal or a fairytale. I think by running away to India, it actually buffered us from the scandal and created the fairytale."

She shook her head. "*You* created the fairytale, love. I have been living the happily ever after ever since."

As she spoke, she picked up a strawberry from her plate. Reaching out, she rubbed it against his lips before she let him take a bite. As his bright eyes dilated, her lower stomach clenched with familiar need. She knew what he liked, and she liked it just as much.

"Careful now, or we shall have to call on Mrs. Higgins to prepare Jason for his day and I shall have to take you upstairs," he said quietly, before he pulled her close for a kiss.

She opened to him, tasting the fruit on his tongue, tasting the desire that made her shiver even after all these years. When they pulled apart, she couldn't help but smile at him wickedly.

"I think we should do that. You see, I have something special for you upstairs in our chamber. A homecoming gift of sorts."

She winked and his eyes went wide. She had never stopped making toys, but now he was her only customer. Her best customer.

"A toy?" he whispered, his fingers finding her thigh beneath the table and sliding up.

She gasped as he stroked her and nodded. "A toy."

Pushing away from the table, he caught her hand and shouted, "Mrs. Higgins!"

As they hurried past the governess and into the house, Cassandra laughed. This future was the perfect one. And she couldn't wait for every day after for the rest of her life.

Although **JESS MICHAELS** came to romance novels later in life than most, she always knew what she liked: ultra-sexy, emotional reads. Now she writes them from her purple office in Central Illinois. She lives with her high school sweetheart husband and two supportive cats. Readers can contact her at http://www.jessmichaels.com.